The Dark Shill

In This Series

That First Heady Burn

True Vermilion

The Dark Shill

A Stack of Sawbucks

The Hillside Roble

The Peroxide Pomp

The Incidental Twin

Brawl in Bardo

The Window-Shade Job

The Convenient Patsy

The Artisanal Grifter

Shrink in the Shadows

Project Chartreuse

From a Desert Playa

The Tired Canary

A Desperate Frame-up

Trail of the Blue Agave

The Saucer-Heads

DAGMARMIURA.COM

The Dark Shill

The Dark Shill

George Bixley

DAGMAR
MIURA
LOS ANGELES

Published by Dagmar Miura
Los Angeles
www.dagmarmiura.com

The Dark Shill

This is a work of fiction. Names, characters, businesses, places, events, and incidents are either the products of the author's imagination or used in a fictitious manner. Any resemblance to actual persons, living or dead, or actual events is purely coincidental.

First published 2018

ISBN: 978-1-942267-59-1

T otally fuckable, Slater thought, assessing the guy's head shot, his bright eyes and beautiful smile, although he wouldn't be telling Della that. Slater was in Della's office, sitting in front of her desk, perusing the file for an insurance claim she wanted him to look into. Della was in her late fifties, dressed today in a plunging cleavage-revealing top, the muted daylight of LA's perpetually overcast June sky diffusing in the windows behind her.

The guy whose photo he was staring at now was dark, darker even than Slater himself, who looked Latin American, like his father. He flipped to the next head shot.

"Which one is the claimant?" he asked Della.

"The blond," she said. "His name is Derek Laird."

Slater studied the photo. Laird was sort of good-looking, blond and blue-eyed, but bland, almost dead-eyed, not evoking the same spark as the guy in the first photo.

"The one you can't tear your eyes away from is Rahim, the sales manager," Della continued. "Laird was the chief accountant at the company—some kind of surgical equipment—until he had a breakdown and filed for long-term disability."

"What's Cudahy Mutual's problem with it?"

"All the medical paperwork came from one doctor. That's not against our policies, but she was subsequently investigated by the DA's office and lost her hospital privileges. We can't deny the claim based on that, but it is suspicious."

"Investigated for what?" Slater asked, looking up at her.

"Writing a startling number of opioid prescriptions," Della said.

"Who noticed all that?"

"The actuaries downstairs. The other red flag for me is that Laird is claiming emotional debility. Why would that happen to an accountant? It's just arithmetic, not IEDs on the side of the road. His salary was huge—$1.5 million per annum—so his insurance benefits are correspondingly huge."

"You're paying him already?"

"The claim was approved a few months ago. The doctor's legal troubles brought it back to my desk."

"So who pays an accountant that much?" Slater asked, cocking his head. "You think the whole thing is a scam?"

Della shrugged. "Maybe. Three people from his company signed statements attesting that he is indeed unable to work. They're the ones in the photos—I lifted them from the company website."

Slater flipped to the next image, a guy with a snaggletoothed smile and long gray hair pulled tight behind his head. It did look like a professional portrait, with him standing in front of an out-of-focus bookcase, and the photographer had captured some hint of his personality.

"The shaggy one is Dave Adler, the company president, believe it or not," Della said, and as Slater turned to the next photo, "Gwen, the HR director."

Gwen was in her thirties, probably, and wore her hair in a stylish tight Afro with swooping blue makeup over her eyes. Also professionally posed, she was in front of the same bookcase as Dave and Rahim. Laird's head shot wasn't part of the series—it looked like a photo from a driver's license or a passport, the kind the cops release to the media when they're looking for someone.

"I didn't put anything in there about the doctor," Della said, "but you'll find her name all over the forms."

"So you want me to see if anything smells bad with these people?"

"That's the idea."

Slater tucked the file into his canvas satchel and rose, looping the strap over his shoulder. "I'll let you know what I find out." Glancing at the dramatic view from her office, thirty-four floors above the Financial District, he said, "How's your beau?"

Della rose and stepped around the desk. "He's getting a little tedious, so I'd have to say he's Mr. Right Now rather than Mr. Right." She raised an eyebrow. "I'd drop him in a hot minute if you wanted to step out sometime."

Slater scoffed. "That's never going to happen, sister."

"So you keep telling me," she said, and grinned. "What about your love life? Are there any boys that you've seen more than once?"

"No way. I'm not falling into that trap."

She walked him to her office door and held it for him as he left.

As he went through the front office to the elevator, Slater ignored the reproachful stare of the receptionist, Crystal or Christine, something like that, dressed in a serious red suit, her bougie hair piled up like ice cream. She didn't like him very much, he knew, but that was her damage, and he pushed it out of his mind as he rode down to the garage.

He handed his claim stub to the valet, and his car, a classic black Thunderbird, soon appeared. When the guy hopped out and held the door for him, he said something to Slater in Spanish. It happened a lot—Slater looked like he should be able to understand, looked like the majority of the people in the city, people with Latin origins.

"Say what?" Slater asked him.

"What year is your ride?"

"It's a '78," he said, pulling a couple of singles out of his jeans and palming them, then passing them to the guy in an almost-handshake.

"It's really beautiful."

"I know," Slater said, setting his satchel on the passenger's seat and pulling the door closed. Even more than the distinctive lines of the classic Thunderbird, he loved the horsepower, effortlessly accelerating up the ramp to the street. The downside was that the car drew a little too much attention for someone in his business. To keep a low profile, he made a habit of parking out of sight of his targets.

It was just a few blocks' drive to his own office in an older part of downtown Los Angeles, the

Fashion District, in a building surrounded by clothing industry suppliers, manufacturers, and retailers. He parked across the street in a surface lot, and as he left, waved to the attendant, who never bothered to check his parking pass, recognizing the distinctive car.

The air was getting hot and muggy as the marine layer burned off, and he appreciated the warm sun as he hustled across in a break between cars. His building contained mostly clothing factories, with porters, seamstresses, and pattern graders coming and going, sometimes hanging around the lobby waiting for gigs. The hallways and the elevator were ancient, the paint peeling and the ragged flooring soiled by many feet over the decades, but at least the clothing industry was basically clean, the machinery small in scale. It rarely got louder than the hum of sewing machines cycling on and off, and in his office, with his door closed, he could hardly hear it.

The space he shared with his business partner was tiny, just three rooms, and only Max's office had a window, but it was working out, this partnering with the big mooky private investigator, and he loved having an office, loved having a place to come to for work. Pushing open the steel accordion when the elevator stopped at his floor, he walked around behind the shaft and admired the new lettering on his office door:

SLATER IBÁÑEZ
MAXIMILLIAN CONROY
INVESTIGATIONS

Stepping into the front office, its only contents a barren desk with a wan *Pothos* on it, he saw that Max's door was open, his bulk hunched over his desk, absorbed in his computer screen. He was in his forties and had a bad haircut, but appropriate for the warmth of the day, he was wearing a blue seersucker suit, open at the collar. Even though Slater regularly wanted to punch him in the face, the guy was easy enough to work with. Max had a PI license and could do things Slater couldn't, and most significant of all, he was pretty competent.

Slater flicked on the lights in his own office, tiny and grubby and windowless. A recent acquisition, intended to make the place feel civilized, was a painting he'd found in a thrift store, of three artichokes in a bowl, hanging on the wall opposite his desk. It was a little faded but still pleasing to the eye. He set his satchel on his desk, pulled out the file Della had given him, and went to Max's door.

"Can you help me with a records check?" Slater asked.

Max looked up and leaned back in his chair, his sidearm bulging under his jacket.

"Let's do it. Who are you looking at?"

That had to be Max's best quality, Slater thought, always willing to get to work, not irritated at the interruption, never waving him off until later.

"Derek Laird," Slater said, and spelled the name, dropping into the chair in front of Max's desk.

Max's thick pudgy fingers danced inelegantly on the keyboard as he dug into the database.

"There are a few of them," he said finally. "Have you got a date of birth?"

Slater flipped through the file to find it and then recited it, calculating in his head as Max typed. Laird was thirty-six. He looked younger than that in his photo, he decided, flipping to it.

"Born in Kansas," Max said, and clicked his mouse, staring at the screen. "No record at all, criminal or otherwise, which is weird."

"Why is that weird?" Slater asked, looking up from the file. "He's not a lowlife."

"Usually people have salary garnishments, moving violations, parking tickets—something." Max looked up at him. "This guy never so much as shoplifted a peanut."

"What else?"

Max looked back to his screen. "No debt, and his credit rating is A. He's a very good boy."

"No surprise that he's got good credit," Slater

said. "He's an accountant, so he should know how to handle money."

"That's all I got," Max said, leaning back in his chair. "Is this for an insurance job?"

"Right. I have to find out if this guy's on the take."

Max nodded. "I'm working tonight too—babysitting some foreigners. We're going to a baseball game, if you can believe that."

Babysitting was easy, steady work, playing bodyguard for the wealthy or the clueless who thought LA was the real-world equivalent of a shoot-'em-up video game. When he put on his poker face and wore his wraparound sunglasses, with his weapon holstered under his jacket, Max looked right for the job, looked like the heavy.

"Take your glove," Slater said. "Maybe you'll save them from getting beaned by a foul ball. Where are they from?"

"Shanghai, or Tokyo, one of those. All women."

Slater chuckled. "Maybe you'll get lucky."

Back in his own office, Slater put his feet up on the desk and pulled the computer keyboard into his lap, looking for Derek Laird online. As Max had implied, there were a few people with that name, but the accountant had no social media presence, not even placeholder accounts. He wasn't old enough to be technophobic or clueless about networking, so maybe he was just an extremely private person. That could help explain the emotional disability.

Pulling out his phone, he checked on Conrad's location. The idiot was at his station, right where he should be. Slater never let himself get emotionally entangled with guys, but somehow with Conrad that had happened, and predictably it had ended badly, with Slater tossed aside like a piece of garbage. But Conrad was a cop, and that meant he had access to resources that Slater needed sometimes, so he maintained the connection. Before they'd broken up, Slater had managed to put a piece of hidden software on Conrad's phone that faithfully reported his location, as long as the device was turned on, and like most people, he never turned it off. It was his own stupid fault, letting Slater see the code he used to unlock it.

If Conrad was at his station, he was probably at his desk, and that meant he could be of use. Slater dialed his cell.

"What do you need, Slater?" he said when he picked up.

"A small favor. A records check on a guy I'm looking into."

"I'm not your secretary," he said irritably.

"Lucky for me," Slater said, raising his voice. "I'd shit-can you in a heartbeat for your attitude."

Conrad chuckled. "Always the charmer. Who's the guy?"

Reaching for the file, Slater rattled off Laird's name and date of birth.

"Let me do it now, while you're on the phone, so I don't have to call you back."

"What a horrible burden that would be," Slater said.

Conrad didn't say anything, but Slater could hear him typing.

"So, he has no criminal record."

"I know that much," Slater said impatiently. "What else?"

"There's really nothing … he has a Social Security number, like everybody. How old is this guy? He's only had it for six years."

"Don't they give those to you when you're born?"

"Nowadays, sure. In the old days you'd get one when you started working."

"I'm sure this guy has been working longer than six years," Slater said.

"Sometimes people get assigned a new one. Identity theft is a big reason—maybe that's what happened to this Laird. He's also got a Kansas driver's license, with an address in Topeka. A PO box."

"I thought you had to have a street address on your driver's license."

"In Cali you do, but maybe not in Kansas."

"He's been working here for years. Why

doesn't he have a California license?"

"You're supposed to," Conrad said. "We remind people to do it on traffic stops. But some people are lazy, and some don't want to change because they can get cheaper car insurance in less populated states. I've seen it before."

Still, it seemed weird for a person with a regular job. "Can you send me an image of it?"

"I'll email it. Is that all you need?"

"For now, yeah," Slater said, grabbing his mouse to click open his email.

"Any other favors you need done? Perhaps waxing your car, or vacuuming your apartment?"

"Fuck you, Conrad."

Conrad chuckled. "Back at you."

Slater ended the call and opened Conrad's email. It wasn't an image of the actual license, just Laird's photo, and in the text of the message, a record number and the information that would be printed on the card—name, address, date of birth. Laird wore the same thin smile as in the head shot Della had given him. Leafing through the file, he compared the printed head shot to the driver's license image on the screen. It was the same photo, his hair tousled in the same way, the same flat blue background. Slater stared at him for a moment. What are you hiding behind those dead eyes?

Time to meet Derek Laird, he decided, and

found his address and phone number in the file. When he dialed, he got a generic voice-mail recording.

"My name is Slater Ibáñez," he told the machine. "I work with Cudahy Mutual Insurance. I need to talk to you about your disability claim."

Hanging up, Slater sighed and flipped through the file again to find the name of the doctor who had signed all the medical paperwork for Laird: Lynn Cheung. A search turned up an office address for her in Downey. That's where Laird's employer was, he remembered, leafing through the documents to double-check.

Online, Cheung's name came up in search results that connected her to a hospital down there, listing her only as "medical doctor," but Della had said she'd been kicked out. A newspaper article farther down in the search results, dated a few weeks ago, named Cheung as one of several physicians being investigated by the DA's office for overprescribing opioids. There was much hand-wringing about medical industry complicity in opioid addiction, but when he checked, there was nothing about Cheung or any of the others being charged with anything, at least not yet. The investigation alone must have been enough to get her booted from the hospital, but she still had an office—she was still practicing medicine.

Slater picked up his phone again and dialed the number for her office. A man's voice answered.

"Is Cheung there this afternoon?" Slater asked.

"Are you having a medical issue, sir?"

"I'm not a patient," Slater said, and before he could continue, the guy spoke again.

"She could squeeze you in later on, say 5:30?" he said. "Were you considering a procedure?"

"That's right," Slater said, sitting up. He hadn't intended to approach Cheung posing as a patient, but this guy was practically inviting him to.

"Where is your primary doctor located?"

"I can tell you all that when I come in," Slater said. "I'll see you at 5:30."

"I'll need your name, at least," he said.

"John Slade," he said. "And you are?"

"Lou. I'm Dr. Cheung's assistant."

Slater ended the call. Using an alias would prevent the guy from researching him, finding out what Slater really did. Slade was an ideal pseudonym, close enough to his own name that it would catch his attention if someone said it. More importantly, he wondered, what kind of procedure had he just claimed to be interested in?

Scrolling through the search results, he soon found out. "Dr. Lynn Cheung—extreme liposuction," one article said. "Drop those stubborn pounds in seconds." Another offered "Affordable liposuction—Dr. Cheung digs deep so you don't have to." He grinned. This was going to be interesting.

Given the afternoon traffic, he'd have to leave soon to make the appointment, he saw, checking the time, but maybe he could find Laird on the same excursion. Anyone with an emotional disability, at least one that prevented them from working, would probably be hanging around home. Pulling up a map on his computer, he found the address Laird had provided on the insurance forms. It was near Tweedy Boulevard in South Gate, right across the river from Downey—he'd drop in on Laird after his appointment with Cheung.

Laird lived in one of those old-school eight-unit apartment buildings, he saw, clicking to a view from overhead and then from the street. What was a guy making that kind of money doing in a run-down one-bedroom? And thinking about it, South Gate was an odd place for a white dude from the Midwest to be living. Like all the big cities, Los Angeles was heavily segregated, and South Gate—really, that whole side of town—was thoroughly Latin.

He got up to open the safe that sat behind his chair, dialing in the combination and twisting the handle, then pulling out the surveillance gear that he'd need. Stuffing it into his satchel, he pulled the bag onto his shoulder and called out, "Bye, Max," as he left.

Once he was in his car he got directions on his phone, which told him to take the 10 and the 710. That seemed absurd, far out of the way, when he knew Downey was a few miles south, no freeways required. But who was Slater to defy the wisdom of the navigation AI? For someone who liked to drive, it was hard to admit that the traffic data made the software better at it than he was. It had proved itself many times, and he always regretted it when he defied its advice. He drove the few blocks to the 10, accelerating up the ramp and deftly slipping into the traffic.

Cheung's office, he found, was in a low-rent strip mall on a tired commercial boulevard that looked like it hadn't changed much since the 1970s, like so many outlying small-town main streets around Southern California. Wedged between a cell-phone store and a nail salon, the sign above the door announced SOUTHEAST LIPOSUCTION CENTER.

Cheung had attempted to make the interior look professional, at least, Slater saw as he stepped inside, with new carpet on the floor and dark wooden office furniture providing gravitas. At the front desk was a guy in his thirties, with a wiry build and thick black Asian hair, a purple blotch under one eye. Not an injury, Slater decided; he'd been born with that. This was Lou—or as the nameplate on his desk read, LIU.

Liu was on the phone, but he glanced at Slater as he walked over, holding up a finger.

"I understand, Mrs. Cutler," he said. "Have you been taking your meds? ... I'll send Dr. Cheung there first thing in the morning. Remind me what room you're in?" He searched his desktop for a pen, lifting stacks of paper and files, and when he found one, wrote something on the pad in front of him. "Try to have a restful night."

After he'd hung up, he consulted his notepad and asked, "John Slade?"

"That's me," Slater said.

"There are a couple of intake forms to fill out before you consult with the doctor," Liu said, and picked up a clipboard, rising and handing it across the desk toward Slater.

"I'm not sure if this is right for me," Slater said, not reaching for it. "I just want to talk to Cheung for a few minutes."

"You might not think you need lipo, but everyone can be thinner," Liu said intently. "Everyone."

"Just let me talk to her."

Liu frowned and hesitated, but he set down the clipboard, then turned and went down the corridor that led into the back.

Stepping closer to his desk, Slater looked at what he'd written on the pad.

Baltimore
512

Baltimore—that had to be the Baltimore Hotel, downtown, not far from Slater's office. Cheung had lost her hospital privileges; was she warehousing patients there instead? Glancing around the ceiling to make sure there were no surveillance cameras, he pulled out his phone and took a quick photo of the notepad, then stepped back, thumb-typing a note to himself with the name of the person Liu had been speaking with—Mrs. Cutler.

Liu reappeared and said, "Come on back."

Walking down the narrow corridor behind him, Slater glanced in an open door to a tiny room with an exam table and other medical equipment—a monitor on a stand, electronics and tubing, an adjustable overhead lamp. No way would Slater let some quack do anything to him in this dank hole.

Cheung's office was windowless but lightened up by a modern desk and luxy dark-red upholstered chairs in front of it, built extrawide, presumably for the kind of people who'd be seeking liposuction. Wearing a white lab coat with her name embroidered on the breast, her straight, dried-out hair spilled over her shoulders like charred straw. She wore thick glasses on her moon-shaped face, and her bulky shape as she rose implied that she might be a potential client for her own services.

"Dr. Cheung, this is John Slade," Liu said, then closed the door behind him as he stepped out.

She greeted Slater briefly, stepping around her desk, and waved to the exam table at the back of the room.

"Hop up and pull off your shirt so I can have a look," she said affably. "Where were you thinking of having work done? Tummy or flanks?"

Slater didn't move. "I wanted to talk about mental health, not liposuction. You worked with a patient named Derek Laird."

"Laird?" she said, and frowned. But Slater saw the spark of remembering strike, and her expression shifted. "You're not here for a procedure, are you."

"I work for the people paying Derek's disability claim."

"I can't talk about my patients," she said, frowning.

"You signed an awful lot of paperwork for him. How is it that an accountant could have an emotional breakdown from his work?"

"I just said I can't talk about that," she said, her voice rising. "There are laws protecting patient confidentiality."

Slater put his hands on his hips. "There are laws against peddling opioids too, but that didn't seem to slow you down."

Cheung's face hardened. "You need to leave,"

she said, and stepped over to her desk, pressing a button on the phone.

"As a representative of his insurer, I have a business relationship with Derek Laird," Slater said. "Confidentiality doesn't apply. When did he first consult with you?"

Liu opened the office door and stepped in. "Is everything all right?"

"Escort Mr. Slade out," Cheung said. "He misrepresented himself."

"If you don't talk to me now," Slater said, "you'll have to do it under oath in a deposition. I suspect you know all about those. Why not make it easier on yourself?"

"Out," she shouted, her face red and contorted.

Liu pulled the door wide, gesturing for him to leave. "Come on, buddy, or I'll call the cops."

Slater sighed and stepped past him, into the corridor and back toward the front office, sensing Liu close on his heels.

"I should have known you weren't here for a procedure," Liu said, once Slater had passed his desk. "You have a very shady aura."

Slater laughed, turning back. "I'm the shady one? You're doing surgery on people in a storage closet in a strip mall."

"Who do you really work for, anyway?" Liu demanded, looking Slater up and down. "You look like a thug."

Moving fast, Slater stepped toward him, and before Liu could react, Slater grabbed his neck, slamming him against the wall. Liu grabbed his arm and tugged, then slapped at Slater's face. Keeping a hand firmly on his throat, Slater grabbed his wrist and twisted it until Liu yelped in pain.

"I'm not a thug," Slater said intently. "Mind your manners, or I'll break you in half."

Assessing the fear in his eyes, Liu didn't seem like much of a threat, despite his pointless struggling. Slater let him go, and walked toward the door.

He'd only gone a few paces when he heard Liu coming up behind him. Slater twisted sideways and ducked, hearing something whiff above his head as Liu lunged at him. Sweeping his boot around under him, Slater threw Liu off balance, lunging to shove him backward. Liu tumbled onto his butt, a heavy object dropping from his hand to the carpet with a thud—a stapler.

"You're trying to split my head open?" Slater demanded. "What kind of animal does that?"

Liu started to get up, but Slater punched him in the face. His head snapped back, and Slater straightened up and kicked him in the ribs. Liu folded in on himself, knees to chin, rolling away.

"Why do you make me do this?" Slater shouted, kicking him in the kidney. "Did you really think you could win this fight?"

Liu groaned, shielding his face with his arms. Watching him for a moment, making sure he wouldn't be coming after him again, Slater glanced around the room, then walked out.

Cheung was shady, there was no question about that, he thought, climbing into the Thunderbird. Della's bean counters were right to flag anything she'd signed.

Pulling out of the parking lot and nosing into the traffic on the boulevard, he thought about Liu. The guy might be able to identify him, despite Slater using a pseudonym, as he'd told Cheung who he worked for. But he'd never call the cops—the last thing they'd want is the authorities poking around their black-market chop shop.

Driving a few blocks, he stopped on a side street and pulled up the address of Laird's apartment on his phone. South Gate was only a few minutes away.

TWO

The apartment building seemed quiet as he rolled past, and old, but not too run-down, certainly not as rough as where Slater lived. He parked up the block and walked back to it. Along the sidewalk out front were three narrow garden boxes, planted with yellow-tinged geraniums. Somebody was overwatering them, killing them with misplaced attentiveness—those things only thrived when they were ignored.

The apartments were on two floors, but all the doors were on the same side, on the right past the little concreted space behind the geraniums where the mailboxes were. A security camera mounted up the gray stucco wall was aimed at the mailboxes, and anyone coming in had to walk through its field of view, but when he went down the side toward Laird's apartment, no other cameras were visible. Laird's door was the third one along, well out of sight of the street.

Slater knocked firmly, and listened, but there was no sound of movement within. Pounding with the heel of his fist, he shouted, "Derek? Come to the door."

But there was only silence. Either Laird was avoiding contact, or he wasn't here. There was one way to find out.

Scanning the corridor again to make sure there were no other cameras, he pulled his own camera out of his satchel. It was built to look like a smoke detector, and even though it was bizarre to have one of those mounted in an outside space, he knew no one would look at it twice, conditioned to ignore such a ubiquitous overhead object. Peeling the paper backing off the sticky base, he reached up to attach it to a crossbeam a few feet away, twisting it so the lens was pointed at Laird's door.

It wasn't a high-end device, storing motion-activated video clips on a memory card, unlike the expensive version that broadcast live video via the cell network. But that lack of connectivity meant it had good battery life, and would function for more than a day, even if it recorded a lot of activity.

Stepping back, he took a critical look at it. Satisfied that it was innocuous enough, he pulled out his hankie and wiped the housing of the device to remove his prints, just in case, then switched it on, careful to stay out of its field of view. Most of his surveillance tech came from some sketchy Russians in Glendale, and most of it was probably illegal for some reason or other, so on the off chance it did get discovered, he wasn't going to make himself easy to find.

Glancing around to make sure he was still unobserved, he walked back to his car.

The map on his phone told him to go back downtown in the opposite direction from the way he'd come, for some reason, and he pulled into the street, following it toward the Alameda Street thoroughfare. He'd have to come back here to retrieve the camera, but he needed to talk to Laird anyway.

Glancing at his phone, he found the number for the concierge desk at the Baltimore Hotel.

When a woman's voice answered, he asked, "Is Miguel working today?"

"I believe so—one moment," she said, and put him on hold.

That would make things easier. Miguel was a hookup from a while back, and Slater had made a point of maintaining the relationship when he found out where he worked—it was useful to have friends inside places like the Baltimore. The sex had been a one-time thing, but like most people, Miguel wasn't allergic to money.

The line clicked, and a familiar voice said, "This is Miguel."

Once Slater identified himself, Miguel said, "Why didn't you call my cell?"

"I don't need to talk to you if you're not at work."

"Nice," Miguel said flatly. "My rates just went up. What do you want?"

"You have a guest named Cutler, room 512. How long has she been there?"

"Let me check," Miguel said quietly, and Slater heard him typing. "Two nights so far," he said finally.

"Is it just her?"

"No one else is listed for that unit."

"Is she using room service?" Slater asked.

More tapping at the keyboard, then Miguel said, "Yeah—every meal."

"Good. Can I deliver her dinner?"

"It hasn't gone up yet, but get here soon. It's that time of day."

"I'll be there in ten," Slater said, and ended the call.

The Baltimore was on the edge of the Financial District, too far to walk from his office, and he hated to valet at the hotel because it was so damn expensive. Instead he parked across the street, in the public garage under Pershing Square.

Strolling through the Baltimore's glam original lobby, with coffered ceilings and craftsmanship that hadn't been seen for a century, he headed downstairs to the staff floor and found Miguel's office. Two women in dark burgundy jackets were working, seated behind desks, both engrossed in phone conversations. One of them looked up at Slater, unconcerned at seeing him step in, and nodded toward the next room. Miguel appeared in the doorway, beaming at the sight of him, and pulled him in. It was a small changing room, with lockers and a bench, like at a gym.

Dark like Slater and a little chubby, Miguel was in his thirties and kept himself clean-shaven, his hair precisely groomed, which was probably a requirement of his job.

"I told the kitchen to hold the tray for 512," Miguel said, standing back to give him the once-over. "You'll need a jacket and tie. Take off your shirt."

As Slater started to undo his buttons, Miguel went to one of the lockers and pulled out a white dress shirt on a hanger.

"I remember that sexy body," Miguel said, admiring Slater's torso as he pulled off his shirt.

"Hey—my eyes are up here," Slater said, glaring at him with mock indignation and taking the white shirt.

"I'm not interested in your eyes, *cabrón,*" he

said, and produced a black clip-on bow tie from his locker, looping it around Slater's neck once he'd pulled on the shirt, then tapping under his chin. Slater tilted his head back so Miguel could fasten the tie.

Slater tucked the shirt into his jeans and took the jacket Miguel produced, in a dark shade of burgundy, like the ones everyone who worked here wore. The gold plate over the breast pocket read MIGUEL.

"It feels kind of loose," Slater said, shrugging his shoulders, and stood still as Miguel adjusted the fit, then tucked his shirttails in more tightly, not shy about standing close and sliding his hands into Slater's pants.

Miguel stepped back and assessed him. "You look fine," he said. "It makes me think we should hang out again sometime."

Slater frowned. "Don't you have a boyfriend these days?"

"Sort of," he said. "You know, it kind of looks weird with the jeans, but hopefully nobody will call you on it."

"Where's the food tray?"

"First, some consideration is in order, sir," he said pointedly.

Slater pulled out his wad of cash and peeled off a twenty.

"You're not going to insult me, are you?"

Miguel said, raising his eyebrows.

"How much do you want?"

"A C-note seems more appropriate."

Sighing, Slater flipped through his cash and pulled out a fifty, offering it to him. Miguel plucked it from his fingers and reached for the twenty as well, but Slater held firm.

"I'm taking a huge risk here," Miguel said, meeting his gaze and not letting go of the bill.

"And I'm overpaying you," Slater said, but released his grip on the twenty.

Miguel pocketed the cash. "The kitchens are this way," he said, and led Slater into the wide main hallway, then around a corner. The place smelled like food and was busy with staff coming and going, moving too quickly and too purposefully even to glance at them. Pausing in front of a swinging double door, Miguel said, "Wait here."

A moment later he reappeared, pushing a cart with a white cloth and a covered tray on it.

"Be careful when you lift the lid," Miguel said. "It's been sitting under a heat lamp."

Slater followed him to a service elevator, taking over the cart and wheeling it inside when the doors opened.

"You're not going to do any mayhem, are you?" Miguel asked.

"Part of your payment is not to ask questions," Slater said, pressing the button for the fifth floor.

"Go left off the elevator," he said, and as the doors closed between them, added, "Bring my clothes back."

When the doors slid open, Slater wheeled the cart down the hall, rolling silently on the heavy carpet, and found the right door. "Room service," he called, rapping sharply on it.

"Come in," came a faint reply.

But it was locked, of course, hotel rooms always were, and he had no way to open it. Why hadn't he thought of that? But groping the jacket, he found a card key in the breast pocket, printed with Miguel's name. When he swiped it, the lock clicked open. Miguel must have put it there, knowing he'd need it. Maybe he really was worth what Slater paid him.

Pushing open the door, he towed the cart in behind him. The room was small, and narrow, typical of the century-old hotel. It smelled funky, like someone hadn't bathed in a while, and the only illumination was the flickering blue glow of the muted television set. Slater flipped on the room light, causing the occupant of the bed to wince and turn away. Her long red hair was unkempt, her skin ashen, and the bed around her was littered with prescription bottles, tissues, magazines.

"Mrs. Cutler?" Slater asked.

"Just park it here beside the bed, and leave the cover on," she said. "I'll get to it, but not just yet."

Rolling the cart up beside her, Slater asked, "How are you feeling?"

"I'm in a lot of pain, dear," she said, squinting at his name tag and adding, "Miguel."

"You had a medical procedure recently, is that right?"

She nodded. "I'm not healing as quickly as I should be."

"Have you seen your doctor?"

"Not since the weekend. I know he's busy."

"He? I thought your doctor was Lynn Cheung."

"That's him." She frowned, touching her forehead. "How did you know that?"

"What does Dr. Cheung look like?" Slater asked.

"Young, handsome, thick hair. He has a birthmark under his left eye."

Slater clenched his teeth. Liu. "He did the surgery at a clinic?"

"He operated on me right here," she said. "It's a simple procedure, he said, no need for a big fancy hospital. Brought all the equipment with him. But I wish he'd come back and look at my incisions."

"Can you show me?"

She frowned. "Besides being a busboy, Miguel, do you also have a medical degree?"

"Just tell me, then—are the incisions swollen, or red, or hot?"

"All three."

"That means you've got an infection. You need to go to a hospital."

"You're not a doctor," she said firmly. "I'm sure of that. I'll do what Dr. Cheung says."

"I don't think he's a doctor either," Slater said, half to himself. "Do you mind if I check your temperature? I just want to feel your forehead."

She shrank back into the pillows. "I think you should go."

"Fine," he said, and stepped back, but added firmly, "Go to a hospital."

Closing her door, he walked back to the elevator and down to the basement. He'd come here to find out more about what Cheung was up to, but this was worse than he'd anticipated.

Miguel was at one of the desks in his office, and rose when Slater appeared, shepherding him into the locker room.

"You got what you needed?" Miguel asked as Slater peeled off the jacket, the tie, and the white shirt.

"Someone dumped her here after she had surgery," Slater said. "I think she's pretty sick— her incisions are infected. Can you call an ambulance?"

Miguel frowned. "You're no doctor."

"That's what she said, but you don't have to be a doctor to see that she's a mess."

"Well, tell her to call her doctor."

"She did, but no one's coming until tomorrow. Dude—you don't want her to die in your hotel."

"I can't get involved," Miguel said, shrugging. "You weren't even supposed to go in there."

Slater sighed, buttoning his own shirt. "Don't worry about it, then. I was never here."

Back on the street, daylight was fading, and the cars had their lights on. Slater trotted across to Pershing Square in a break in the traffic. Before he went down the stairs to the parking garage, he stopped for a minute and phoned Conrad, getting his voice mail.

"Can you arrange for a welfare check?" he told the machine. "It's urgent. This woman had surgery, and the medical people abandoned her at the Baltimore. She's got an infection but refuses to go to the ER. Her name is Cutler. Room 512." Before he hung up, he added, "You did not hear this from me—consider it an anonymous tip."

———◦———

There was never anything to eat at Slater's place, and near home, in gritty Westlake, he stopped at a *pupusería,* one that he knew made some without meat, wrapped in rice instead of corn masa. He ate perched on a stool at the counter, and thanked the woman in broken Spanish when he left.

It was almost dark as he pulled into his alley,

nosing the Thunderbird under his garage door as it rose, then waiting for it to roll down again before he went upstairs. The ground-floor tenant in front of his garage was a cell phone store, so everything was heavily reinforced against break-ins, which suited Slater just fine.

The private garage was the best thing about this place, he thought, trotting up the two flights to his shabby little apartment. It was technically a one-bedroom, but the main room was essentially a kitchen at one end and a sofa and recliner at the other, with the bedroom off to one side. It wasn't dirty, but the carpet was worn and blotchy and stained, the thrift-store furniture sagging and tired.

As he came in, he eyed the almost full fifth of bourbon sitting on the kitchen counter. It was too early for that—guys came before booze. A good night for Slater featured both, but things worked best when guys came first.

Early evening light still filtered in the dingy windows, with a view of a strip of sky above the building across the street, but there were always guys on the prowl. Pulling his boots off and loosening his belt, he stretched out on the sofa and pulled his phone from his pants. Before he opened the hookup app, though, he set it on the carpet for a minute, rubbing his eyes. He could rest, he decided, just for a few minutes.

Waking in the dark, he wasn't sure if he'd heard a noise or if it was just the chaos in his own mind. He listened for a minute, hearing only the constant dull roar of the city outside, then scrabbled for his phone. It wasn't that late yet, he saw, and Conrad had texted:

> Passed your tip along. Patrol headed to the Baltimore now. Call me later if you want me to follow up with them.

Whatever happened to Mrs. Cutler, it wasn't going to be of any use to Slater, but he texted Conrad a quick "Thanks" anyway, then opened the hookup app. Digging through the faces and torso pics, before he'd even found anyone interesting, he got a message from another user:

> U hawt. Fuck me. Ur place. Ready now.

Slater grinned and looked at the guy's profile. He was a bit angular, sunken cheeks and hooded eyes, and made phony pouty lips for the camera, but he was fuckable, he decided. The no-nonsense approach made up for a lot—it saved a lot of time. Slater never tolerated the wishy-washy back-and-forth thing for long, but it was a cumulative waste of time, as it happened a lot.

Typing his address in response, Slater added:

> Nowhere to park around here. Take a rideshare.

Getting up from the sofa, he put the bourbon away in a cupboard, then picked up the clothes strewn on the bedroom floor, dumping them in the bottom of the closet. Pulling the sheets up on the bed wasn't really equivalent to making it, he knew, but it looked a little cleaner. Unbuttoning his shirt, he changed into a tight white T-shirt. He looked better in it, and there was less chance that he'd smell sweaty.

A sharp knock took him to the front door, and the guy broke into a smile when Slater opened it.

"You look like your picture," he said.

You don't, Slater thought, but held his tongue. The guy was at least a decade older than his profile implied. He seemed nervous as he stepped inside, his eyes darting around.

"What's your name?" Slater asked.

"Rocky," he said, taking in the space. "What a dump."

"Yeah, I hear that a lot."

Rocky turned back to him, looking surprised, as if, in the few moments he'd been looking away, he'd forgotten that Slater was standing there. "How are you doing?"

Slater folded his arms, assessing him. The guy was fidgety, agitated, definitely high.

Rocky blithely walked into the kitchen. "So where's your bed? Let's get busy—I want to rip your clothes off." He turned back to Slater, again as if noticing him for the first time. "Hey."

Slater sighed. Rocky wasn't a big guy, and he could probably manage him if he got out of hand, but he wasn't up for this. "You have to leave."

Rocky's face fell, his expression rapidly shifting from dismay to anger. "Excuse me?" he demanded.

"I can't do this," Slater said. "You have to go." And added emphatically, "Have to."

"What, I'm not pretty enough for you? Too swishy, maybe?"

"Swishy guys are fun—tweakers, not so much. You're way too high."

"I am not tweaking."

Slater scoffed. "Tweakers always say that. I can't keep up with a meth-fueled libido. I need to sleep later."

"So you're just wasting my time?" Rocky said, raising his voice. He looked around, and beside the sink, within arm's reach, snatched up a tumbler, then hurled it at the wall behind Slater, where it smashed with a glassy crunch.

"Meth makes you erratic," Slater said calmly. "Did you ever notice that?"

"Fuck you," he spat, and heaved open the front door, slamming it against its stop.

Slater followed him into the hall, grabbing his collar and spinning him around, then punching him in the face, twice in rapid succession. Rocky tumbled to the filthy carpet, landing on his butt and his elbows, yelping in surprise. A dark red line trickled out of one nostril, and he dabbed at it, then studied his finger.

"What was that for?" he asked, more sober now.

"You shouldn't break my stuff. It's going to take me an hour to clean that up."

The door next to Slater's opened, and at the periphery of his vision Slater glimpsed wispy gray hair and rheumy eyes. He didn't have to look; he knew it was Grace, well into her eighties and incapable of interfering in this. Even if she could, he knew she wouldn't make trouble—he'd helped her out more than once, and they had an understanding.

Rocky got to his feet, his initial surprise morphing to murder in his eyes, and hurled himself at Slater, grabbing fistfuls of his T-shirt. Slater punched him underhand in the gut and pushed him to the floor. Slater's shirt slipped out of Rocky's fingers as he went down, and he pulled up his knees, covering his belly, groaning. Slater kicked him hard in the side.

"Why do you make me do this to you?" Slater shouted, then kicked again.

Rocky rolled away and got to his knees, then wiped the blood off his lip with the back of his hand. It was like he wasn't feeling it, the pain of the gut-punch and the blows to his back, inured to it by the meth. He got to his feet, unsteady at first, glaring.

"If you come at me again, tweaker, I'll break your nose," Slater said, fists balled at his sides. "It's your decision."

"Is everything OK, Slater?" Grace asked.

"Just taking out the trash," he said grimly.

"This prick just assaulted me," Rocky said, waving his bloodied hand as proof.

Grace took a timid step into the hall. "From what I saw, it was self-defense. I'm certain I saw a blade in your hand."

Rocky looked from her to Slater, then his arms dropped, and his eyes went dead. He'd made his decision. Turning to open the door to the stairs, he trotted down.

Slater waited, listening to his uneven foot-falls as they faded, and finally looked at Grace, and smiled.

"Did he ruin your shirt?" she asked.

"I think it'll be OK," Slater said, glancing down and smoothing it out. The white cotton was marred with a dark red smear from Rocky's bloody finger.

"Take it off now, and soak it in cold water before it sets," she said, and furrowing her brow, "You know, I may have taken your newspaper the other day."

"I don't get the paper. It must have been a mistake."

"That's what I thought too." She smiled. "Have a pleasant evening, dear."

"Good night, Grace," he said, and went back into his apartment, carefully stepping around the shards of glass. At least the carpet was thin enough that it would be easy to find it all.

Stepping into his boots to protect his feet, he pulled off his shirt and threw it in the sink, as Grace had advised, running the water until it was swimming. He picked up the big pieces of broken glass and then vacuumed up the detritus. It took a minute to figure out how to use the vacuum cleaner, as it was really here for Rosa, who cleaned up and did his laundry. It went quickly once he finally got it plugged in and running.

Tweakers were so freaking self-indulgent. The guy just wanted to use Slater, like a tool, a mirror for his ego. Why did they always think other people couldn't tell they were high? After he'd finished cleaning up, he decided against scrounging up someone else; it wasn't that late, but he'd had enough human interaction for one night.

He pulled the bourbon out of the cupboard and filled one of the surviving tumblers, then dropped in an ice cube. This was the moment, he knew, anticipating the taste, the best moment of the whole day, relishing it as it scorched his palate.

The most predictable lover ever, it never let him down, never acted inconsistently, never smashed his dishes. Standing at the counter with his eyes closed, he took another long sip. The tweaker, he could live without, but he could never forgo this sublime part of his life.

Draining the glass, he poured another, then stretched out on the sofa, turning on the radio. The program was upbeat late-night house music, and he could feel his mind sinking into it, unwinding, relaxing, sweet oblivion.

 THREE

Waking in his bed, naked and alone, he looked around his bedroom. He had no memory of how he got here. Had there been a guy? Thinking about it, gradually waking up, he remembered: Grace, and the broken glass. What a waste of time. Forcing himself to sit up, his head throbbed, but not too badly, not the worst he'd been. On the way to the bathroom he spied the bourbon bottle on the counter, startlingly a lot emptier than it had been yesterday.

Back in the kitchen he looked for food, but found only a skinny jar of olives and a larger one, almost empty, with a couple of pickles in it. Fishing out a few of the olives, he ate them over the trash, spitting out the pits. In the cupboard were some saltines, the kind of two-cracker packets that must have accompanied a long-ago takeout order, and he ate those over the sink, munching absently. His T-shirt was still there, swimming in murky shallow water. Grace was right, he saw when he wrung it out, the bloodstain was gone. Hanging it on the shower rail, he looked at himself in the bathroom mirror. He should probably shave, he thought, running a hand through his thick black hair. It could wait another day, he decided, and pulled on his jeans and a clean shirt.

Swinging his satchel over his shoulder, he locked the deadbolt and headed down to his garage. The smoke-detector camera outside Laird's apartment had to be swapped out for a fresh one, and he unlocked the cabinet that stood just past the nose of the Thunderbird, heaving open its heavy doors. Some of his surveillance gear was kept here, and even though it looked like an ordinary storage cabinet, it was heavily armored and bolted to the floor. Grabbing another faux smoke detector and stuffing it into his satchel, he locked it up again and climbed into his car.

It took him a minute riffling through the case file to find the details on Laird's company. The guy wasn't working there anymore, he knew, but the colleagues who'd backed his claim in writing were there, including that hot sales manager.

Ganesh Medical Supply, it was called. The address was in Downey, not far from Cheung's clinic, and the map on his phone said it was less than half an hour's drive, mostly on the freeway.

———•———

Far from a lively part of town, Ganesh's neighborhood was low-rise, with wide streets and lots of parking. It looked like nothing new had been built in decades. Not in decline, necessarily, but it certainly wasn't booming, or even dynamic.

The street number for the business was posted on a tall fence of closely spaced vertical steel bars that ran around the site. Despite the heavy fence there was no gate, just a gap that served as a wide driveway from the street. A yawning parking lot fronted a squat commercial building, emblazoned GANESH, that stretched back on the long lot. It was definitely a workday, as half the parking spaces were occupied, and Slater pulled into an open one near the driveway, far from the building.

Heaving his satchel onto his shoulder, he walked toward the door under the Ganesh sign. Three Mexican *washingtonias* grew on the little patch of grass between the parking lot and the front of the building, their fanning fronds lazily fluttering in the warm breeze at least thirty feet up. These had been here for a while, and someone was taking care of them—no hanging dead petioles, no seeds scattered on the ground.

The double front doors were made of glass,

and he caught sight of the receptionist before he pulled them open. She had dark Latin features and flat-ironed hair, and looked up at him as he stepped inside.

"Can I help you?" she asked amiably.

Slater rattled off his credentials, adding, "I need to talk to Dave Adler."

"Let me check whether he can see you," she said, and rose from her chair.

"I'm going to talk to him eventually," Slater said sharply. "Stall me if you want, but you'll find I can be persistent."

The woman looked startled. "Give me a minute," she said, and walked down the hallway, away from her desk.

Slater looked around the lobby while he waited. It was a workplace, functional and basic, with a couple of plastic chairs near the door, a poster of an abstract painting in a cheap frame, and the receptionist's counter. Salespeople needed a showier environment—that part of the business must happen somewhere else.

The receptionist came back and said, "Follow me."

They walked toward the back of the building, the wide hallway passing a series of windows onto what looked like a very clean workshop, empty now but with machinery that gave it an industrial vibe. Farther along the woman stepped into an office, wood-paneled and comfortable but not ornate. Sitting behind a cluttered desk was Dave, as in his portrait wearing his dingy white hair tied tightly at the back of his head. He was in his sixties, probably, and looked scruffy to be the head of a company, unshaven and wearing a short-sleeved shirt with a green hibiscus-flower print.

Dave rose and smiled at him, the creases around his eyes deepening, and extended a hand across his desk. Not unfuckable, Slater decided, if the opportunity came up. Slater shook his hand, then pulled off his satchel when the guy waved at a chair. Dave gave him a subtle once-over as he sat.

"So why is Cudahy Mutual concerned about approving Derek Laird's insurance claim?" Dave asked.

"They've already approved it," Slater said, "and they're paying him, apparently. My role is routine research. Just to make sure we understand everything correctly."

Dave nodded. "What can I help you with?"

"I was wondering why your company is called Ganesh? Was the founder from India?"

Dave smiled. "I founded the company. I developed my first product when my mother was convalescing from an illness. It was a simple medical device that made her quality of life a lot better. It's shaped a little like an elephant's trunk, which made me think of the god Ganesh. It's a urinary stent, inserted adjacent to the kidney."

Slater held up a palm. "That's all I need to know. You started in medicine, or engineering?"

"I trained as a nurse. I couldn't stay in that field, for various reasons, but several times with patients I saw the need for medical devices that didn't exist yet."

"There was a workshop back down the hall. You manufacture your products here?"

"Only the prototypes. Large scale production is done overseas."

Slater nodded. "And you're title is president, not CEO?"

"The company isn't publicly traded. It's still just me. I employ a lot of people, but I like to be in charge."

"What kind of employee was Derek Laird?"

Dave leaned back in his chair. "He saved me a lot of money with the tax man. He also figured out some Wall Street voodoo way to make money off the money people pay us, while we're holding it, before we have to pay our suppliers. Unequivocally, he has an amazing mind for numbers."

"So he was worth his absurdly high salary," Slater said, holding his gaze.

"You get what you pay for, right? He was good at what he did. It wasn't all salary either—a lot of what we paid him were bonuses."

"When was his last day here?"

"I have no idea. You'll have to ask Gwen in HR. She deals with all that. It wasn't that long ago, I don't think."

"Can I look at his office?" Slater asked.

"Derek worked from home. We have a few employees who do that. I don't love the idea, but in his case, it worked out fine."

"He didn't have an office here?" Slater said, raising his eyebrows. "How often did he come in?"

Dave gestured helplessly. "For meetings and tax time, I'm sure. Personally I've only ever talked to him on the phone."

Slater frowned. "You just said you liked to be in control."

"I'm talking about the things we make." He picked up a small object from his desk that looked like a twisted piece of brass and twirled it around. "The gizmos. That's what I'm passionate about. I delegate the staff management and the accounting stuff to more capable people."

Which means you're clueless about what's going on in your own business, Slater thought, but held his tongue. "So you never had a face-to-face with Derek Laird."

"We communicated plenty, whenever it was necessary. Everything is digital nowadays, so he didn't really need to be here. He was almost like an outside contractor."

"Just to be clear," Slater said, "even though you signed a form and a written statement about his disability, you never actually observed the disability yourself."

Dave sighed. "I sign a lot of things. I'm a big-picture guy, and for a lot of the minutia, I just do what I'm told."

"Who told you to sign off on Derek's disability?"

"Gwen," he said, raising his eyebrows.

"I need to talk to her," Slater said, half to himself, rising from his chair.

Dave stood up too. "Is that all you need from me?"

Slater met his gaze. "For now," he said sharply, and walked out.

In the lobby, he asked the receptionist, "Where's Gwen's office?"

Slater knew where it was before she spoke, as her eyes darted to the hallway opposite the one he'd just come from.

"I should tell her you're here first," the woman said.

"I'll save you the trouble," Slater said, walking off.

A plaque that read GWEN ROBERTSON—HUMAN RESOURCES was posted beside a door that hung half open, and Slater pushed his way inside. Her office was spacious, much larger than

Dave's and comparatively dramatic, with bright-blue carpeting and white space-age furniture. File cabinets lined one side, behind a white table with four chairs around it, upholstered in the same shade as the carpet. Gwen was behind her sprawling tidy desk, with a white mug for pens, a white phone; even her computer was white. She had the same heavy eye makeup he'd seen in her portrait, the same perfectly coiffed Afro, today wearing a pin-striped gray suit. She was on the phone, and her eyes narrowed as he stepped in.

"I see him," she said, and hung up the handset.

"Gwen," Slater said, stepping toward her desk.

"You're the insurance guy," she said, and looked him up and down. "It doesn't look like you spend much time in an office. What is your job, exactly?"

Not waiting to be invited, Slater dropped into one of the white oyster chairs facing her desk, setting his satchel on the floor at his feet.

"It's all about information," he said. "What kind of employee was Derek Laird?"

She sighed and looked away, folding her hands on her desk. "Derek was more than competent. Management was happy with his work."

"Meaning Dave?"

"Correct."

"Laird worked from home. Was that unusual?"

"He negotiated that." She shrugged. "It worked fine."

"Were there signs that he was having an emotional breakdown before he stopped working?"

"I can't really get into specifics. I'm bound by confidentiality rules."

"Whatever your rules are," Slater said sharply, "he's taking Cudahy Mutual's money, and I need to determine whether the claim is legit."

Her eyes widened. "Is that being questioned? I can assure you, he was completely debilitated when he left us. He sat in that very chair crying like a baby."

"So he did come into the office sometimes. Dave said he'd never met Laird face-to-face, which struck me as odd."

She nodded. "Dave's extremely busy, and his passion isn't accounting. Derek is quite the introvert, but still, I'm surprised they were never here at the same time. Derek came in for meetings, and to manage the year-end reporting process."

"So how is it that an accountant can become disabled from work? I would think accounting was a low-stress activity."

"I see a whole gamut of stress in our employees," Gwen said, leaning back in her chair. "One guy in the workshop cut his thumb to the bone, blood everywhere, and he just taped it up and laughed it off. He was back at work the next day showing off his stitches." She grinned. "So it's all relative. Derek was dealing with large sums of money, which I know I would find stressful. You're obviously not an office worker—what stresses you out?"

"Deception," Slater said flatly.

"In any case, it doesn't really matter what impact his work had on his disability. The policy states that it doesn't have to relate directly to employment, just that he be employed at the time."

Interesting that she knew that, Slater thought, watching her. HR's job was to protect the company, not look out for the employees.

"Why are you so attached to him getting paid?" Slater asked.

"He's a decent guy, and I hate to see him suffering."

That sounded a little thin, but he let it go. "What about his private life? Did he have a girlfriend, boyfriend, kids?"

"Again, I can't really gossip about that."

"I can find out if he declared any dependents on his taxes," Slater said sharply. "Do you really want to make me go to the trouble?"

Gwen sighed. "He's not married. There was a girlfriend a while back, but I think that's finished."

"Is Rahim here today?"

"Rahim didn't really work with Derek," she said, and frowned. "Is there a specific reason you want to talk to him?"

"He signed a statement attesting to Laird's disability," Slater said intently, "just like you did. Where's his office?"

"On the opposite side of the building. The first office past reception. But let me see if he's in."

Slater picked up his satchel and walked out, down the hall and crossing the lobby, ignoring the receptionist, who watched him closely as he passed but didn't speak. Walking into Rahim's office, he found the guy standing beside his desk, holding the phone's handset to his ear, looking at Slater, his eyes wide. He was about Slater's height and had a sharp haircut, his shiny dress shirt and black pants showing off the pleasing contours of his body.

Slater waited for him to get off the phone, glancing around the office. It was similar in scale to Gwen's, with lots of floor space, and instead of a table and chairs there was a plush red fainting couch and two wing chairs around a coffee table, all of it colorful and stylish, the kind of showy furniture designers always chose. It made sense that his office was flashy—the sales guy was the one bringing in the money.

Rahim said "OK" a couple of times, listening to someone talk, and finally, impatiently, "I got it." Replacing the handset, he flashed Slater a smile—beautiful, brilliant, it made him want to squint, or avert his gaze. This guy could be dangerous—weaponized, that smile could enthrall anyone.

"Slater Ibáñez," Slater said.

Concern had flitted across Rahim's face when Slater had first walked in, but now he spoke with the bluster of a salesman.

"An insurance man," he boomed. "I feel safer already. We can talk over here." Rahim stepped over to the lounge furniture and gestured to one of the wing chairs, sitting in the other and crossing his legs, looking perfectly relaxed.

"So you know why I'm here," Slater said as he sat down.

Rahim gestured widely. "It's a small office. Word gets around."

"I like the fainting couch," Slater said, nodding to it. "Do you find much use for it?"

Rahim guffawed. "I don't faint very often, if that's what you mean."

"Tell me about Derek Laird."

"I didn't work with him directly," he said, his levity fading.

"You signed off on Laird being disabled. You must have known something about him."

Rahim waved his hand. "I did that because they needed three statements to file the claim. We were friendly in the office. I know he was having some problems."

Three different stories so far, Slater thought.

Dave said he was never here, Gwen said he came in for year-end, and now Rahim had hung around with him in the office. They might all be lying, but as a salesman, this guy had guile in his DNA.

"Did you have firsthand knowledge that he was legitimately disabled," Slater demanded, "or did you just sign a piece of paper to get it off your desk?"

"I know he was debilitated," Rahim said quickly. "Toward the end, his work was getting sloppy. I'd get reports with whole sections missing."

Another lie, either his or Gwen's; she said they didn't work together.

"What about his family, his home life?" Slater asked.

"I don't know anything about that," he said, frowning.

"You were friends in the office, but his private life never came up?" Slater said, raising his eyebrows.

"He didn't talk about it," Rahim said, spreading his palms. "Maybe there was a girlfriend at one point. I don't remember exactly."

"OK," Slater said, watching him.

"I hope you won't cut him off, Slater. He was a decent guy," he said, and flashed that smile again, holding his gaze.

Was, Slater thought. Past tense. The fact that Rahim had remembered his name, and the glow of that smile, were almost enough to make him overlook that. He wanted to believe anything Rahim said, felt biologically compelled to believe him. The guy must be incredibly successful at shilling the medical schlock.

"You know, you could totally be a model," Slater said.

Rahim laughed loudly again, his head tilting back. "Maybe in India. Here they want them blond and blue-eyed."

"Not everyone here. I'd hit on you before I'd go after any albino Nordic."

"Are you hitting on me?" Rahim said, his eyebrows rising.

"I'm glad you can tell."

"I'd like to talk about that," he said, leaning forward. "It's almost noon. Can I buy you lunch? There's a funky sports bar near here."

Slater hadn't expected the guy to call his bluff. He watched him for a moment, then sighed. "It's not a good idea. I have to keep my dick out of my cases."

"I thought Derek Laird was your case," Rahim said, unfazed.

Slater hesitated, but said, "It's hard to argue with that."

"So let's go," Rahim said, jumping up and

moving to his desk, where he scooped up his keys and his cell phone.

Slater stepped into the hall, pulling on his satchel as he waited for Rahim to lock up his office, then followed him through the lobby.

Once they were outside in the parking lot, Rahim said, "Carpool?"

"I'll follow you," Slater said, and walking toward his own car, watched him climb into a black BMW. The guy had a flashy job; he could be forgiven for driving a flashy car.

Rahim drove fast, changing lanes without warning, but Slater was able to keep up. Following the Beamer into a strip mall, he parked beside it and climbed out, opening the trunk and stowing his satchel.

"Sweet ride," Rahim said, looking over the Thunderbird, and Slater walked with him toward the bar. It looked like a chain joint, bland and greasy and corporate.

Before Rahim could pull open the door, Slater stopped. "So what are we going to do in there? Ogle the waitresses? Flirt some more? The only vegan thing on the menu is going to be french fries."

Rahim frowned. "You're vegan?"

"You got a problem with that?" Slater demanded, raising his voice.

"Dude, chill," Rahim said, raising his palms.

"You just don't seem like the type."

Slater wanted to gut-punch him, and saw alarm in Rahim's eyes as he stepped closer, reaching for him, and grabbed his shoulders, leaning in and locking their mouths together. Startled and stiff at first, Rahim went lax and kissed back, lingering in it, his hands dropping onto Slater's waist. The guy was really good at it, responsive and intent. Why did that piss Slater off even more?

"You know," Rahim said, pulling back, "I'm not all that hungry. My house is near here."

"Let's go," Slater said quietly, and dropped his hands.

They climbed into their cars again, and Slater followed the Beamer down the boulevard and into a residential neighborhood. Rahim pulled into the driveway of a bungalow, and Slater parked on the street out front. The house dated to the 1960s, probably, he saw as he climbed out, and nothing about it looked old or worn, with a newish paint job, even drought-tolerant landscaping in what would have originally been the front lawn—coyote brush, and Catalina fuchsia; hummingbirds loved that stuff.

"Where is this, like Santa Fe Springs?" Slater called to Rahim as he walked up the driveway.

"Downey," he said, and opened the front door, stooping to scoop up the mail.

Slater admired his butt as he rose, then

glanced around. The dining table and living room furniture, all part of the main room, looked like it came from a design catalog, and there was no clutter anywhere. Even the bookshelves at the side of the room contained color-coordinated antique hardbacks, undoubtedly set up by a designer and not meant to be read.

"You're Ismaili," Slater said.

Rahim was at the kitchen counter, depositing the stack of mail and his keys. "How do you know that?"

"Why else would you have a portrait of the Aga Khan on the wall?"

"Oh, man—my mother would love you."

Slater studied the black-and-white image, hung between the foyer and the main room. "I guess he was kind of hot."

Rahim came up behind him and wrapped his hands around Slater's chest. "You only need to focus on me."

Slater turned around and pulled the knot out of Rahim's necktie, then unbuttoned his shirt, admiring his torso. Running his hands into Rahim's hair, he kissed him, again getting lost in it, his cock swelling in his jeans.

"Come on," Rahim said finally, leading him to his bedroom, where he pulled Slater down onto the bed and started undressing him, unbuttoning his shirt and loosening his belt.

Soon they were both naked, and Rahim was rock-hard. Slater massaged his cock.

"Aren't you going to fuck me?" Rahim demanded, scowling, an edge in his voice now.

"If you have condoms."

Rahim reached for the nightstand and found one, ripping it open and rolling it on Slater's swollen cock. Sliding his hand between his legs, Slater gently massaged his way inside him, breathing hard.

"I'm doing this for you," Rahim snapped, out of nowhere, anger in his eyes.

"I get it," Slater said, and moved to kiss him, shut him up. This guy had something mentally weird going on with sex, but he didn't need to get into it.

It didn't take long to penetrate him, as Rahim was ready, and Slater slowly built up the tempo of his thrust, one arm cradling Rahim's chest. The expression in Rahim's eyes was off, more like rage than ecstasy. Slater buried his nose in his hair and came, shuddering, then grabbed Rahim's still-hard cock, stroking him to climax, with Rahim groaning and arching his back.

Afterward, stretched out on his back, catching his breath, Slater eyed him. There were dark shadows under Rahim's eyes, making him look overtired. They hadn't been there before. Slater put a hand on his cheek, gently rubbing his skin, then looked closely at his thumb.

"Guy-liner," Slater said. "I thought that was your natural coloring."

Rahim chuckled and wiped his cheek, his amicable demeanor restored. "At least it was subtle enough that you couldn't tell."

"You don't need it. You're beautiful either way."

He rolled toward Slater and kissed him briefly, then sat up. "Do you want to shower?"

"Maybe just give me a towel," Slater said.

Rahim threw it to him from the doorway of the bathroom, then went back in. Slater heard the water start running. After he cleaned up and got dressed, he looked around the house. The furniture fit the place perfectly, as he'd noticed when he'd first come in, and it was all consistent, but looking closer, really thinking about it, the stuff was generic, and had no character—it just looked good because it was new. Was Rahim that devoid of personality, or was he hiding something?

Riffling through the stack of unopened mail on the kitchen counter, there was a letter from an online investment broker, some self-evident junk mail, a window envelope from a health insurer, and two letters from Downey Orange Growers Bank. He'd never heard of it. Most of the small banks had been wiped out in the last big economic crisis, but obviously there were still a few around. The bank's logo was actually the fruit, perfectly spherical and colored an unnatural lurid electric hue in this printing, with two green leaves still attached. You shouldn't be taking the leaves when you picked citrus fruit. Slater scoffed. Had these people ever seen a real orange growing on a tree? The juiciest ones weren't the color of carrots; those were hard and dry, meant to be shipped out of state. You wanted the soft yellow ones, hard to distinguish from lemons except by their shape.

Rahim's keys and cell phone were on the counter too. The guy was either careless or had been in a big rush to get Slater into the sack. He picked up the phone and pressed the power button, but it was protected by a pass code. Setting it down again, listening to the shower running, he considered saying good-bye. Rahim will figure it out, he decided, and left.

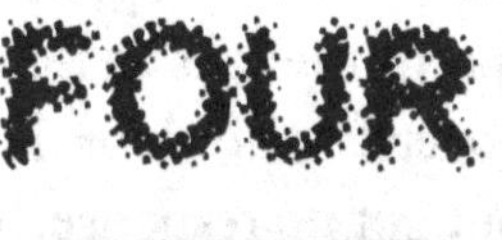

FOUR

L aird's apartment was a short drive, west across the 710 and the concrete drainage channel that had once been the LA River. As he pulled up on the place, he saw a portly woman in tight jeans and a stretchy top come out of the building, walking slowly because she was holding a toddler's hand. She looked Latin, which is who he expected to find in this neighborhood, rather than people like Derek Laird.

Slater parked near the corner and waited until the pair had passed him before he climbed out and retrieved his satchel from the trunk. Remembering the camera aimed at the mailboxes, he put on the blue ball cap he kept in the trunk, embroidered with the interlocking letters that named the metropolis, pulling the brim low over his eyes before he walked to Laird's door.

No one was around, so he reached up and pulled down his smoke-detector surveillance camera, glad that the sticky foam stayed with the device and not on the beam. Stuffing it into his bag, he peeled the waxy paper off the base of the new one before he put it up, in the same spot, rotating it to point the lens at Laird's front door.

Stepping over to the door, he banged on it with his fist, but got no response, heard no movement. "Open up, Derek," he shouted. "You have to talk to me."

The woman he'd seen earlier on the street walked into the corridor, now minus the toddler. She spoke to him rapidly in Spanish, but all he could pull out was *"Hola."*

"Lo siento," he said. *"No comprendo."*

"Can I help you?" she said, suspicion in her eyes.

"That depends. Who are you?"

"I'm the manager. Who are you looking for?"

"His name is Laird. He rents this apartment."

She crossed her arms. "Looks to me like he's not home."

Slater pulled a twenty out of his pants, letting her briefly see what it was before folding it up and palming it. In a building this size, she wasn't a full-time staffer, just a tenant who could call a plumber or reset the breakers in exchange for reduced rent. Stepping toward her, he offered his hand. "When's the last time you saw him?"

The woman hesitated but took the bill, not looking at it, tucking it into her pants pocket.

"I never see the guy," she said, shrugging. "I guess he keeps to himself."

"When did he move in?"

"Before I got here." She looked thoughtful. "Do you think we should do a welfare check?"

"Can you do that yourself?" he asked. It would be an easy way for Slater to get a look inside.

She shook her head. "It has to be the police. I can give them the key."

"Don't bother, then. In this weather, if there were a dead body in there, you would have smelled it already."

She wrinkled her nose, and Slater said, "Do you ever see anyone else coming or going?"

"His girlfriend, sometimes. Not for a few weeks."

"What's her name?"

"I never talked to her. She's black, with round black hair," she said, waving her hand around her head, "and lots of makeup."

Slater nodded. Gwen. If she was sleeping with Laird, it explained her interest in him getting paid.

"Listen," he said, shifting up the brim of his cap. "You're overwatering your geraniums."

She frowned. "What?"

"In the boxes out front. Ease up on the water."

She didn't reply as he stepped around her, walking back up the block to his car.

When he climbed in, he ditched the ball cap and texted Max:

In the office today?

His reply came as Slater was pulling onto the street:

Headed there in an hour or so.

The mapping software took him downtown on yet another unfamiliar route, on surface streets he'd never driven before. Still, it felt the same as anywhere on this side of town—dusty low-rise Latin neighborhoods, with small independent shops crowding the storefronts, discount retailers, diners, gas stations, garages. Cruising the boulevards here was like the looping background in an old cartoon, the same features appearing again and again.

Slater parked across the street and went up to his office, dropping his satchel on his desk and flipping it open to retrieve the smoke-detector camera. After he gingerly pulled out the memory card, he plugged in the device to recharge the battery, then slid the card into his computer. It only recorded video when it sensed motion, and there were four clips. The first one he clicked on was in black and white, time-stamped late at night, and the action that had triggered it was a moth flying near the lens, a fluttering brilliant white blob in the infrared glare. Two other clips were the same, just flying bugs, and the last one was in daylight, revealing a bird hopping around on the concrete in front of Laird's door. Slater sighed and erased the memory card. Maybe the idiot wasn't even living there.

As he was sliding the card back into the camera, he heard keys rattling at the front door. Max was wearing the seersucker again, Slater saw, when he appeared in his office doorway.

"How were the women from Shanghai?"

"They're actually from Nagoya," Max said. "One of them is famous over there, because a couple of people recognized her and approached us."

"So you actually had to guard their bodies."

Max grinned. "I did, although it was pretty low-key. They loved the game—those gals know more about baseball than the umpires do. What are you working on?"

"Can you check some records for me?"

"Let me get settled," Max said, and Slater soon followed him into his office.

"What have we got?" Max said, scooting his chair up to his desk and pulling his keyboard closer.

"Gwen Robertson," Slater said, "and I'm not sure if the 'Gwen' is an abbreviation or not. I don't have a date of birth, but she's in her late thirties, I'd say, and local."

Max spent a minute typing and peering at his screen. "There's only one Gwen who's the right age. She's thirty-six. Lives in the Arts District."

"That fits," Slater said. It was a trendy neighborhood, and based on how Gwen dressed and how she had decorated her office, she was a trendy woman. He stepped around the desk and stood beside Max's chair to look at the screen, thumb-typing her address and date of birth into his phone.

"She's also a bad driver," Max said, pointing to the screen. "Four moving violations in six years. … and look at this: misdemeanor domestic violence. She got probation."

"No other details?"

"I can only get the charges and the disposition."

"Domestic violence could mean anything. I wish I could find out what she did, and to who."

"Your cop friend could find out," Max said.

"I'm not sure it's worth it," Slater said grimly. "Thanks, buddy."

Back in his own office, he swung his feet up on his desk and checked Conrad's location on his phone. He was at his station, the moron, probably sitting on his duff, slack-jawed and drooling, staring into space. He'd been there since noon, the app said, which meant he wasn't going anywhere for a while yet.

The charging indicator on the smoke detector camera had turned green, so he disconnected it and stuffed it into his satchel, then called goodbye to Max and headed down to the street. Rampart Station was a short drive, and he parked out front, double-checking the tracking app to make sure Conrad was still here before phoning him.

"I'm at work, Slater," he said when he picked up.

"What a happy coincidence. I'm right outside. Come out and talk to me."

"I'm busy," he insisted.

"Doesn't your union negotiate coffee breaks? Wipe the drool off your chin, zip up your fly, and come outside."

Conrad hung up on him, but Slater knew he'd come out. Climbing out of the Thunderbird, he waited on the sidewalk in front of the steps, dappled with sunlight and the long shadows of the end of the day.

Conrad soon appeared, wearing his uniform but not his ballistic vest. Dark-haired and swarthy, perfect skin, that perfect jawline—he was such a beautiful man. Catching sight of him, he waved Slater over to the accessible ramp, away from the building's entrance.

"I think you like seeing me," Conrad said, folding his arms.

"I like the way your uniform fits, although I'm not a fan of the ugly part poking out the top of it."

"You drove over here just to insult me? What do you want? And don't try your lame-ass blackmail thing. There's nothing you could do or say that would embarrass me in the slightest."

"Whatever lets you sleep at night," Slater said. To motivate Conrad he often used the threat of distributing photos of them having sex. Slater didn't have photos like that, of course, but Conrad didn't know that.

"I help you because you're my friend, Slater, and because I know you're usually doing the right thing," he said. "Despite your ham-fisted approach."

"Keep telling yourself that," Slater said flatly. "I get that you have a fragile ego. You have to protect it as best you can."

Conrad sighed. "I never followed up on the welfare check at the Baltimore, so I don't know what they found."

"I don't care about that," Slater said, waving impatiently.

"So what do you want?"

"A criminal record. I know this woman was convicted of misdemeanor domestic violence, and I need the details."

"Text me the name and the dates. I'll see what I can find out."

"Oh, you'll do it, toots," Slater said, "and you'll like it too."

Conrad scoffed. "Why can't you admit that you have no power over me? It makes me think you're the one with the fragile ego."

"Fuck you, Conrad," he said, and walked back to his car. Freaking idiot. Why did the guy have to be so abrasive? Climbing in behind the wheel, he texted him Gwen's name and the date of her domestic violence charge.

Slater hadn't eaten very well for days, and felt a hankering for a substantial meal. Despite the evening traffic, he drove over to the strip of restaurants on Fairfax where there was a vegan Ethiopian joint. He sat at a table in the back, far from the windows but with a view of the room.

Halfway through his dinner, eating the spongy *injera* with his hands, he felt eyes on him, and spied a woman, around his own age, trying to catch his eye, smiling at him when he noticed her. What was it about Jewish women? They gravitated to him, especially the Israelis, their finely tuned radar somehow able to sense that Slater was part of the tribe, technically Jewish because his mother was. He nodded to her in acknowledgment and shifted his focus back to his plate.

The sun was long gone when he drove home,

sated, wondering if he needed to arrange a hookup. On the kitchen counter in his apartment was the bottle with a few inches of bourbon in it, its unopened twin still in the cupboard. It felt so inviting. Maybe Rahim had been enough sex for one day. He poured a tumbler of the heady amber and slammed it, then poured another, dropping in an ice cube, smiling to himself at the luscious sweet burn in his throat.

Flicking off the room lights, he sat on the sofa to pull off his boots, then stretched out, starting a *Sasquatch Search* podcast. It's not something he'd ever do himself, tramping around the woods looking for signs of the great cryptid, but the quest took him out of the everyday, away from this grimy city. Dropping his phone on the carpet, he embraced the liquid gold slowly seeping into his brain.

His phone rang, silencing the podcast, and he scrabbled for the glowing screen in the dark. Conrad, he saw, and picked up.

"So your new friend is a real charmer," Conrad began. "The DV was for causing corporal injury, and it got reduced to misdemeanor domestic battery. Gwen choked out her girlfriend—in front of the girlfriend's kids. Someone called an ambulance, but the girlfriend was just out, no permanent damage. Your target claimed that the girlfriend fainted, but the kids told the real story."

"You have to be pretty angry to choke someone unconscious," Slater said. "It sounds like Gwen can be vicious when she needs to."

"There's only one incident on record, but these people always reoffend."

"Are you still at work?" Slater asked.

"Just leaving."

"Yeah? You can swing by, if you want."

The line was silent for a moment before Conrad spoke. "You know I can't do that," he said quietly. "You know we're no good for each other."

Slater closed his eyes, feeling the blood pounding in his temples. "I know that." He knew he shouldn't have said it. Feigning indignation, he added, "I can't believe you'd even try that with me. Go home and find a twinkie to blow you. The Valley's full of them."

Conrad scoffed. "You're slurring your words."

"I'm not drunk, but yeah, my inhibitions have been lowered. It's the only reason we're still talking. It's totally messed up that you'd try to take advantage of that."

"Oh, Slater." He sighed. "I should go. Lay off the bottle and get some sleep."

Slater ended the call. It was so irritating that the guy never got upset. He hated that about Conrad, the consistency, the frustrating predictability. Taking another slug of bourbon, he resumed the podcast. Following the narrator and his posse into the woods, a place with no freaking Conrad, it started to feel like he was there with them, and he sank into it, the humid darkness, the canopy of evergreens, the deep forest.

———◆———

He was alone, he knew, waking in his own bed, as the apartment was quiet, and it took a minute to remember what had happened last night. Yeah, he'd been alone.

Finding a granola bar in the kitchen cupboard, he peeled it open, biting into it. In the bedroom his phone rang, and it was his most dreaded ring tone: *"No wire hangers … What's wire hangers doing in this closet when I told you no wire hangers, ever?"*

"Damn it," he said, slapping down the granola bar, and went to the bedroom to grab it. "What do you need, Doris?" he demanded.

"I wanted to ask you to lunch," she said affably. "I'm going shopping downtown."

"What are you, a 1950s housewife?"

Doris laughed. "I'm just not sure what kind of restaurant would have your vegan food."

Slater sighed audibly. "How about Mexican? There's a decent place on Seventh with both options."

"A vegan compromise. That sounds perfect."

Ending the call and leaning on the counter, he munched on the granola bar. The last person he wanted to see today was his mother. She'd become even more irritating since he'd discovered that she'd been communicating with Conrad. It drove Slater crazy because he had absolutely no control over it, and he had no idea what they were conspiring about. One thing was certain—it had to be about Slater.

In the bathroom he glared at himself in the mirror, running a hand over his cheek, examining his stubble. If he was going to see Doris, he needed to shave.

Once he was dressed, he backed the Thunderbird out of the garage, driving a few blocks on the 10 and then down Alameda, to Tweedy Boulevard and Laird's apartment. Parking up the block, he didn't bother to put on his ball cap; the manager had already gotten a good look at his face. Scanning the corridor to make sure he was alone, he spent a second swapping out the smoke-detector camera, replacing it with the fully charged one.

Once again he banged on Laird's door, to no response. He checked the window next to the door, the blinds still tightly drawn, and couldn't see an alarm sensor. It made sense—most people renting a cheap apartment wouldn't install an alarm system. Walking around the other side of the building, he found the trash bins and the parking spaces, Dingbat-style, several feet lower than the ground floor and partially under the structure. Counting from the far end, he figured out which were Laird's windows, and climbed up on top of the largest Dumpster to check. The blinds were closed here too, and he wasn't very close to the windows, but from this vantage point he could tell there were no sensors on this side either. Satisfied, he hopped off the Dumpster and walked back to his car, heading back to Alameda Street and downtown.

It was too far to walk from his office to meet Doris, as he'd arrive all sweaty, so he decided to bite the bullet and pay for parking in the Historic Core, which was exorbitantly priced on weekdays.

The restaurant was in a converted street-level retail space, the marble floor and century-old decorated plaster ceiling intact and restored, elegant wrought-iron stairs leading up to the bar at the back. Walking in, he saw Doris being led to a table, several shopping bags in hand. Petite and shorter than Slater, she was letting gray streaks show in her dark hair these days. As he approached, she said something to the host, touching her forearm. The young woman nodded sympathetically and gathered up all the shopping bags, toting them over behind her little desk. Even though Doris was retired, she still had her classroom skills, bringing out the best in people, convincing someone with plenty of other work to do to help her out and take charge of her stuff.

Joining Doris at the table, Slater bent down to kiss her hello, then sat on the bench beside her.

"Don't you look handsome," she said, reaching around and giving his shoulder a squeeze.

"I always look like this," he said, frowning.

"That's what I'm saying—my handsome son."

The waiter approached, asking Doris, "Something to drink?" And looking to Slater, "And for your brother?"

"Oh, stop," Doris said emphatically, leaning toward the guy, but Slater could tell she was loving it.

"Just a Corona," Slater said, frustrated with the charade.

"I'd better stick to water," Doris said, and once he'd gone, said to Slater, "Drinking in the middle of the day?"

"It's just a beer with lunch," he protested.

"I wanted to talk about that. Do you drink every evening, or only on the weekend?"

"That's none of your damn business."

"You kind of made it my business," she said.

"What are you talking about?"

Doris paused as the waiter set Slater's beer on the table and poured water for them both.

"You don't remember calling me late Saturday night?" she said, glancing at him sidelong.

Studying her, he saw that she was serious. He could feel his heart pounding, his face heating up. Why would he have done that, and what had they talked about?

"I don't remember calling you."

"I'm not surprised," she said. "You were slurring your words."

What the hell had he said to her? He wanted to ask, but that would be admitting he'd been out of it, proving her point.

"I know there are some good places around town to dry out," she said. "Maybe we can look into it together."

"I don't need to dry out," he snapped, "and I don't need to quit drinking, because I don't have a drinking problem."

"Are you sure about that?" she said, and then looking toward the front entrance, broke into a smile and waved. "There he is."

Slater followed her gaze and saw Conrad walking in, wearing his civvies, chinos and a dress shirt that flattered his torso. A stupid big smile on his face, he stooped to kiss Doris hello.

"How *are* you?" he asked, briefly holding her hand.

"What the hell are you two up to?" Slater demanded, glaring at him.

"Nice to see you too," Conrad said, and sat across from them.

Slater turned to Doris. "What's going on?"

"Calm down," she said, tapping the back of

his hand. "I've been planning to have lunch with Conrad. I knew you'd freak out if you found out about it." She waved her hands in the air for emphasis. "Now you know exactly what we're up to, because you're sitting right here."

Slater looked at Conrad, pointedly dropping his eyes to his shirt. "You look like a cop trying to not look like a cop."

"Ease up," he said, his brow furrowing. "It's my day off."

The waiter stopped by, and Conrad ordered a lemonade.

"Nice place," Conrad said, glancing around the room.

"I like the atmosphere," Doris said, "and they even have the vegan food."

"Your mother is so thoughtful," Conrad said, looking at Slater.

"I picked the place," Slater said.

"Really?" Conrad frowned. "You're not usually a fan of high-toned joints."

Slater wanted to tell him to go fuck himself, but he wasn't going to do that in front of Doris. He pressed his lips into a hard line, suppressing his reaction.

"It seems quiet, though," Doris said.

"That's because it's not tweaker time yet," Conrad said.

Doris leaned toward him. "What's that?"

"When all the tweakers finally wake up after a long night of partying. They've got the munchies, and they swarm the restaurants. It's usually around two or three."

"Even on a Thursday?"

"It happens every day," Conrad said.

"You're right, though," Slater said to her. "It's more pronounced on the weekend, and more noticeable in WeHo."

"How are things going with your DV?" Conrad asked him.

"What's a DV?" Doris asked. "And stop talking in code."

"We'd been talking about a domestic violence charge. The perp is a woman in Slater's case."

"Stop talking about my case," Slater said irritably.

"A DV perp," Doris said, raising her eyebrows. "She sounds like a bad girl. What did she do?"

"The arrest and conviction are public record," Conrad said, "but I can't really talk about the specifics." He shrugged. "It's nothing worse than what Slater's done to me when he's upset."

Slater shot him a murderous look, and Conrad raised his eyebrows, tacitly asking, *What?*

Doris was already looking at the menu. "Ooh, they have *mancha manteles*. This was a good pick."

Slater sighed and picked up his menu. After they'd ordered, he listened to their idle chatter, sometimes chiming in, trying to act civilized.

When she'd finished her main dish, Doris set her fork down and leaned back on the bench. "So why did you two break up?"

"My god, woman," Slater spluttered.

Conrad spread his arm languorously along the back of the neighboring chair. "Slater once said that I'm like his kryptonite."

"Interesting," she said, glancing at Slater. "That implies that you sap his power."

Slater scoffed. "Sure—him and what army? He couldn't disempower me with a tool belt, a Humvee, and three days to practice."

Ignoring him, Conrad said, "I think he meant that I make him soft."

"That's not a bad thing," Doris said. "It's a shame things didn't work out between you two."

"You don't get a vote, Doris," Slater said, raising his voice.

"Settle down, now," she said, touching his arm.

"At least it gave me the opportunity to meet you," Conrad said, with a sappy smile. "That makes it all worthwhile."

"Such a charmer," she said.

"Charming?" Slater demanded. "That's a stretch. All he does is work and play video games."

"What's wrong with video games?" Conrad said.

"I wish you'd spent more time on those when

you were younger," Doris said, "and less time getting in trouble."

Slater folded his arms. "I don't know what's going on with this little cabal of yours, but I don't like it one bit."

"We're just having lunch, sweetie," Doris said. "There's no hidden agenda."

Slater looked from her to Conrad. He wasn't so sure that was true.

They all walked out together, Slater stopping at the host's desk to retrieve Doris's shopping bags for her, then once she had hold of them all, kissed her good-bye. Ignoring Conrad, he walked back to his car.

Conrad really was good with her, he thought, driving the few blocks back to his office. At one point, when they'd still been together, Slater had called him "the mom whisperer," to Conrad's great delight. Still, he made Slater look bad by comparison. He hated that Conrad was so goddamn nice. Maybe that's why the whole thing was so infuriating—Doris would have been a lot happier, a lot better off with a son like Conrad.

FIVE

Up in his office, Slater pulled the memory card out of the smoke-detector camera and slid it into his computer. The same as yesterday, the first two recordings were spurious fluttery moth hits, but then the one that had taped at 5:36 this morning, still in twilight but clearly identifiable in the infrared-lit black-and-white image, made his heart pound. He sat up and leaned closer to the screen. It was Gwen, walking up to Laird's door, twisting a key in the deadbolt, and going in. It was just a few seconds, and just the back of her head, but that haircut was unmistakable.

Slater stared at Laird's closed door as the last few seconds of the video ran out, then clicked on the final recording on the card, stamped 5:52 a.m.

Gwen stepped out the door, looked both ways, then locked the deadbolt and moved out of frame. Rewinding it, he froze the image as she came out of the apartment, black-and-white and blurry but unmistakably Gwen. Slater stared at her, standing there with her side-eye expression, dressed for work. They needed to talk.

After he copied the videos to his cloud storage, he went down to his car and headed to Ganesh's offices, taking the freeway, driving hard. Walking up to the front door, he scanned the cars in the lot, wondering which one was Gwen's. The parking block nearest the door was stenciled with THE BOSS. No one was parked there now, but that must be for Dave. In the next space was a white Mercedes convertible with the top up. That fit Gwen's image, and of course she'd be parked right next to the boss. Glancing around to make sure he wasn't being observed, he photographed her rear plate, then went inside.

Ignoring the receptionist, he turned right, toward Gwen's office.

"Can I help you?" the woman called after him, but Slater was soon at Gwen's door.

Gwen looked up from her computer screen, startled, as he strode in.

"Where is Laird?" Slater demanded.

She frowned. "How would I know?"

"Don't give me that bullshit," he said, hands

on his hips. "I know you know. Unless I can talk to him, he's not going to be on disability for long."

Gwen stared at him, and Slater saw the wheels turning as she thought it through, calculating her next move.

"Let me call him," she said finally.

Slater gestured to her desk phone. "Go ahead."

"I have to do it privately. Confidentiality issues."

"I need you to give me his number. The one he put on the insurance forms was bogus."

"I'm sure it wasn't bogus," she said. "Maybe he typed it wrong, transposed the digits or something."

Slater shook his head. "I feel like I'm getting the run-around. I know you know more than you're telling me."

"Derek is an emotional wreck right now," she said, holding his gaze. "You have to make some allowances for that. Let me look into it, try to talk to him, and I'll text you a number for him before the end of the day. Deal?"

"Fine," he said flatly, and then pointed a finger at her. "But if you're fucking with me, I don't care who you're sleeping with, or how violent you are—I will burn you to the ground."

She scowled, clearly not intimidated. "There's no need to attack me. I'll do what I can."

Too calm for a desk jockey, Slater thought.

She's seen things get rough before.

"I need to talk to Laird's colleagues here," Slater said. "Whoever worked with him."

"There are a couple of people in accounting, I guess. Let me see if they're around."

"No way." Slater shook his head. "Give me their names, and I'll find them myself. You're not going to play intermediary."

Gwen eyed him, considering that. "Jasmine or Claudia," she said finally. "Both of them collaborated with Derek."

"Where are their desks?"

"Accounting is in the cube farm down the hall."

Slater turned and walked toward the door.

"Try not to scare anyone," she called after him.

Farther along, as promised, was a big open room with two rows of cubicles. The first one he came to bore a nameplate that said JERRY WILSON, and inside was a guy in his mid-twenties, wearing a necktie and heavy dark-rimmed glasses.

"Hey, Jerry," Slater said, standing in the entrance to his space. "I'm looking for Claudia."

Jerry turned toward him, startled, and briefly glanced down at Slater's jeans. "I don't think she's in today." He rose and beckoned Slater to follow, leading him farther in among the workspaces. "This is her desk. See? No signs of life."

"What about Jasmine?"

In the cubicle across the aisle, a woman rolled her chair into view. "I'm Jasmine," she said, giving Slater the once over. She was still in her forties, maybe, and dark, Indian or Middle Eastern, her hair in a comely style and wearing a dark blue dress with a silver pin.

"Gwen said you might have a minute for me," Slater said, and glanced at Jerry, standing there wide-eyed, as if it were any of his business. "Is there somewhere we can talk?"

"I guess I can take the time, if Gwen sent you," she said, her brow furrowing. She got up and led Slater back into the hallway. Besides Jerry's, several other sets of eyes were on them as they left. No one had any privacy in a space like this, Slater realized.

Farther down the hall, Jasmine led him into a lunch room, with an array of round tables, a fridge, windows overlooking another part of the parking lot. It was better outfitted than his apartment—a microwave, a snack machine, and an industrial-scale coffee maker. The room was deserted, understandably, with the end of the workday approaching.

"Do you want a coffee?" Slater asked.

"No, but help yourself." She sat at one of the tables. "I'll warn you, though, it's been sitting there since this morning."

Slater poured himself a steaming mugful

from the carafe and sat across from her.

"What's this about?" she asked, glancing at his mug.

"I work for one of Ganesh's insurers. We're covering Derek Laird's disability. I have some questions."

"For me? Like what?"

"You worked with him?"

She cocked her head noncommittally. "He wasn't my supervisor—or anyone's supervisor, for that matter. Derek was like a managerial accountant. I'd prepare all my statements and billing electronically, and he'd process it all. That was his thing, the high-level work, compiling material from all the departments. He did a lot at tax time, although he always worked from home. Everyone said he was a whiz at juggling the tax code."

"He never came into the office?"

"He might have, but I don't think I ever saw him."

"What about for year-end reporting?"

Jasmine frowned. "He was never here for that. There are a couple of other people who work from home. It's hard to keep track. People always said Derek was reclusive. I guess it's no surprise that he had a breakdown. I know he worked late nights—I'd regularly get documents from him time-stamped three or four in the morning. Doesn't that sound like someone who's bipolar?

They're not very good with the circadian rhythm thing."

Slater sipped at the acrid coffee. "Dave seems to think he was good at his job."

"He was fast, and skilled at organizing things, and good at finding other people's mistakes. He wouldn't fix them; he'd always just send an email that said 'Something's wrong here,' and he was usually right. Derek made mistakes too sometimes, but not very often." She grinned at the memory. "When he did screw up, though, it was always a lulu."

"What do you mean?"

"Well, one time we were dealing with a client named Steele. It's the name of the company, from the family name, right? But Derek misunderstood it as 'steel.' We do buy medical-grade steel, in small quantities, for several of our products. Anyway, he categorized everything to do with Steele as an input, something we were buying. And once something is miscategorized, it starts to snowball. Subsequent transactions are impacted and mislabeled. It took forever to untangle it all."

"That sounds like a pretty boneheaded mistake," Slater said.

"Or maybe the kind of mistake you'd make if you were distracted, or working furiously in the middle of the night." She grinned at him. "Brilliant people often have big blind spots, don't you find? Frank Lloyd Wright couldn't manage money. His staff had to keep him on a budget, giving him a few dollars to spend every day."

Slater watched her. Accounting brilliance wasn't the same as artistic brilliance. And what kind of gifted mind didn't know how to spell *steel*? "Did anyone else work with Laird directly?"

"Claudia, but she didn't know him any better than I did. I think she told me once that she had lunch with Derek when she first started, or when he first started, so at least she met him. I never did."

"Who replaced him when he went on disability?"

"We brought in two new people to pick up the slack. Even two full-timers are slower than Derek was on his own."

Slater nodded, sipping his scorched coffee. "If he wasn't in the office very often, I suppose you can't really comment on the extent of his disability."

"I know he stopped working suddenly. Everything was normal, cooking on all the burners, and then one day, nothing. It must have been a serious psychological break."

"What about Gwen?" Slater asked. "How is she to work with?"

Jasmine's face clouded. "No one really works with that woman. Her loyalty is to Ganesh, not the staff. Of course there's a lot of hard feelings toward her."

"HR people always side with the company," he said. "Is there more to it than that?"

"I'm not one to gossip," she said, lowering her voice and glancing toward the doorway. "But last year she pressured one of our team to quit because he was underperforming. If someone quits, they can't get unemployment insurance—you're only eligible if you get fired. Employers have to pick up part of that cost, so they don't want to fire anyone. Anyway, this fellow knew that, and refused to resign. Finally Gwen told him, 'Don't come back.' So he didn't, but it wasn't in writing, and of course she told the unemployment office that the guy had abandoned his job. It was really cruel, if you ask me."

"Still, I'm sure most employers would handle it that way," Slater said.

"Maybe, but you asked about Gwen specifically. She didn't have to push it that far. It illustrates her ruthlessness."

"What about Rahim? What's he like?"

Jasmine shrugged. "I don't know him. I do know that he's skilled at spending money—I handle his expense account, but not his sales accounts. All those people in sales are flashy, don't you think? He'll take three or four of his buyers on a junket to Vegas or Hawaii and lay out ten or twenty grand in a weekend."

Slater nodded, then drained his mug and stood up. "Thanks for your time."

Jasmine rose too. "I feel sympathy for Derek, in some way. He was always perfectly polite, and consistent in his work. I hope you'll give him the benefit of the doubt."

"First I need to track him down. I don't suppose you know where he's staying since he went on disability?"

She shook her head. "I don't know anything about his personal life."

Slater walked back past the accounting area, glancing into Gwen's office as he went by. The door hung open, but the room was empty, the lights off, the only illumination coming from the windows. He stopped in the doorway and looked around. Almost everything was white or blue, even the art on the walls. The chairs around the table were by one of those mid-century designers, although he didn't know the name, white frames with blue upholstery. More significant were the file cabinets. It would be useful to look in those, given Gwen's resistance—she had invoked employee confidentiality, but it felt more like obfuscation.

Walking out to the lobby, he spoke to the receptionist, the same dark-haired woman who'd been here yesterday. "Is Gwen around?"

"You're the insurance guy," she said, frowning.

"She's gone for the day. Can I take a message?"

"It's fine," he said, turning away. "I have a meeting with Jasmine right now."

If Gwen left her door open, it meant that everything of value was locked up, almost certainly in those cabinets. Stepping into her office, he checked the hallway to make sure he hadn't been observed, then flicked on the room lights and closed the door. There was no lock on it; he needed some other way to prevent someone walking in on him.

The chairs around the conference table were too short, and Gwen's desk chair was on wheels, so that wouldn't work. Finally he settled on the table itself. It was oblong, and when he picked it up and flipped it sideways, legs in the air, it fit nicely under the doorknob, at a perfect angle to the floor. Slater kicked hard at the edge of the table that was resting on the carpet, jamming it tighter under the knob. No one was coming through that door now without a fire ax.

Checking the file cabinets, they were locked, as he knew they would be. But most people hated carrying big bunches of keys around, especially someone as concerned about her appearance as Gwen was. They could be in her desk, but he found the drawers unlocked when he pulled on them, and they contained nothing beyond office supplies, paper, and forms.

The keys had to be somewhere else, but they were definitely here, he decided. No way was Gwen hauling a keyring around like a janitor. Slater looked in her pencil cup, and under the blotter, then scanned the bookshelves behind her desk. A set of keys could conceivably be hidden behind the books, but would she go to that trouble? She'd have to rearrange her library twice a day. In the middle of a shelf, between two bookends, stood an African figurine, an elongated woman's head with stylized knobby hair. He smiled. That had to be it.

It looked like it was made of dark-stained wood, but when he picked it up, it was cool to the touch, and heavy—stone, maybe, or ceramic. And there they were, sitting underneath in the object's hollow base, a ring of little keys. It was so obvious, once he'd looked around. She could have locked them in her stupid desk and walked around with just the one key. But no, that need for convenience and a light handbag was her downfall.

Taking the keyring over to the cabinets, he scanned the labels on the drawers. What he wanted wasn't going to be in RECRUITING, or TRAINING, or EEO, whatever the hell that was; it had to be in STAFFING. The third key he tried worked in the lock, and he pulled out the top drawer. These were definitely the personnel files.

Rahim's dossier was here, and it was fat. Slater pulled it out, flipping through it. Most of the documents were performance reviews. Dave consistently rated him highly, it seemed, flipping through the pages. Another document revealed his salary, which seemed surprisingly low. But salespeople were usually on commission, so he probably earned a lot more than that.

Stuffing the folder back, he saw Jasmine's, almost as thick as Rahim's, and in the next drawer Jerry Wilson's, so thin that he must be a new hire. But after reading the tab on every folder in all three of the staffing drawers, he found nothing for Derek Laird.

Standing there with the keyring in his hand, considering whether to open the other cabinets, on the off chance he might find something useful, he knew that his time was up when the doorknob rattled. Someone tried to heave it open, and then there was a knock. A muffled woman's voice called, "Gwen?"

Slater sighed. All he'd learned was that Laird's file had been removed. Quietly closing the drawer, he locked the cabinet and went back to Gwen's bookshelf, placing the keys where he'd found them, under the sculpture. Back at the door, he listened for a moment, but Gwen's visitor had moved on. After heaving on the legs of the table to free it from its wedged-in position, he set it back where he'd found it, lining up the feet in the depressions they'd left in the carpet. Walking out of the office, he left the door ajar, at the same angle as when he'd arrived, glancing both ways before heading toward the lobby.

The receptionist stepped into the hall before he got there. "Were you in Gwen's office?" she demanded.

"I was talking to Jasmine," he said, scowling at her and flashing his palms but not stopping.

"Jasmine left already," she called after him. "What were you up to?"

"I got turned around," he said over his shoulder.

Glancing back as he pushed out the front door, he saw that she was headed toward Gwen's office. It didn't really matter what she thought he'd been doing; he hadn't taken anything or done any damage.

Rather than getting into the traffic right away, Slater pulled onto the street and parked a few blocks away. He needed to think, and make some notes, and he pulled his tablet out of his satchel, resting it against the steering wheel.

Of the three people who had aided Laird with written testimonials, Gwen and Rahim had definitely lied to his face. Gwen wasn't afraid of him, and it definitely felt like something hinky was going on with her. It was harder to be objective about Rahim. Why had he slept with the guy? It was so stupid, breaking his own rule about keeping his dick out of his cases. What about Dave? Slater spent a minute digging for information about him online, finding his generic bio on the company website, and eventually finding his home address. Surprisingly, Dave lived in Downey too. The overhead view and the street photos of his house revealed that it had nice landscaping, and a pool out back, and plenty of windows, but it wasn't ostentatious, and certainly wasn't a mansion. What were all these Anglos doing living in this part of town?

There was a map from the last census that he'd seen, showing details down to the neighborhood level. Pulling it up now, it showed one dot per person, color-coded by ethnicity. Instantly he saw that his assumptions were wrong—parts of Downey were actually pretty well integrated. Dave wasn't at all out of place here. But Derek Laird's neighborhood in South Gate was a different story, he saw as he dragged it into view on the map. It was all one color, almost completely Latin.

His phone rang, interrupting his thoughts. Slater glanced at the caller ID and picked up.

"I had fun yesterday," Rahim said. "I wish you'd stayed longer. Will you let me take you out to dinner?"

Slater did want to question him, but not at a restaurant. "No on dinner," he said, "but I'll fuck you again, if that's the ultimate goal."

"Wow—so brutal. Can we at least talk a little first?"

"Sure, I'll talk to you, Rahim. Where are you?"

"My place."

"Do you have any food there?"

"There might be some leftover chicken thing."

"I'll stop and get a burrito. Do you want one of those?"

"That sounds almost as good as going out for dinner. Yeah, bring me a burrito."

Hanging up and searching on his phone, Slater found an Anglo Cali-fresh place nearby, a chain that he knew made vegan fare at a spice level that wouldn't startle Rahim's Americanized palate.

When Rahim opened his front door, he was still dressed for work, wearing a blue shirt and a tie, and he pulled Slater inside, locking lips with him, running his hands down Slater's back.

"Want something to drink?" he asked, finally pulling away.

"Let's eat first," Slater said, handing him the paper sack with the burritos.

Rahim went to the kitchen and found a couple of dinner plates, which he set on the dining table, then pulled out the burritos and put one on each. As Slater watched, he ripped off two pieces of paper towel and set them beside the plates. His hosting skills didn't equate to the image created by his furniture—luxurious dining didn't happen here; this was a guy who ate out a lot.

A muted chime came from the kitchen counter, and Rahim stepped over to pick up his phone. As he typed his code to unlock it, Slater was close enough that he could see the numbers. Rahim didn't even try to conceal them. It was easy to remember: Rahim's house number, but with the digits in reverse order. Rahim thumb-typed a quick text and absently set the phone down again.

"Shall we?" he said, eyeing Slater and pulling out one of the dining chairs.

Sitting adjacent to him and unwrapping his burrito, Slater said, "Tell me about Dave. What's he like?"

"Great guy to work for," he said, his mouth half full, and paused to swallow before he continued. "Totally hands off. As long as we're selling, I have free reign."

"And you understand medical equipment well enough to market it to the right people?"

Rahim shrugged. "It's not that complicated."

"Did you ever see evidence of anything shady? With Dave, I mean."

"Dave's pretty easygoing," he said, and frowned. "I can't imagine him doing anything illegal. I'm sure he doesn't want that kind of trouble."

"What about Gwen?" Slater said.

Concern flitted in his eyes, and he took another bite of the burrito. "What about her?"

"What's she like? Who's she sleeping with?"

"She has a girlfriend. They live in the Arts District."

Slater raised his eyebrows. "That's a pricey neighborhood."

"So what? They're trendy, and I think her partner is a high earner."

"Was she ever involved with Laird?"

"Romantically? I doubt it. She's been with the same woman as long as I've known her."

"What about you? Did you ever fuck Derek Laird?"

Rahim watched him for a moment. "You're kind of coarse, you know that?"

"That's not an answer."

"I wasn't sleeping with him. I hardly knew the guy."

That wasn't what he'd said yesterday, Slater thought, watching him eat. He couldn't even keep his story straight overnight.

"How are your inquiries going?" Rahim asked.

"Nowhere. I need to talk to this knucklehead Laird. I can't seem to track him down. Gwen was supposed to put me in touch with him, and now I'm going to have to deal with her too."

He frowned. "What do you mean, 'deal with her'?"

"She told me she was going to do something for me, and she didn't do it. I'm not going to let that go."

"Such a hard-ass," he said, balling up the foil wrapper and wiping his hands on his sheet of paper towel.

"If you're finished," Slater said, "let's get to the main event."

Rahim grinned and got up, leading Slater to his bedroom, pulling off his tie as he walked. Slater started to unbuckle his belt, but Rahim took his hands.

"Let me do it."

Pulling Slater's belt out of its loops, he slid his hands into the back of his jeans, leaning in and kissing him, his mouth firm, insistent.

"You're so beautiful," Rahim murmured, pushing Slater's pants down and grabbing his ass.

Slater took hold of his chin, pulling it up, looking him in the eye. Rahim looked surprised, and Slater kissed him again, pulling him onto the bed and helping him undress. Rahim grabbed his cock, squeezing it until he was rock-hard, then reached into his nightstand to retrieve a condom, rolling it on Slater.

Shoving Rahim's knees up, Slater gently pushed his way into him, breathing hard, and Rahim gasped at the intensity, closing his eyes and wrapping his hands around the back of

Slater's neck, pulling him closer. As Slater built up to pounding him, Rahim again had an off-putting expression on his face—anger, maybe— teeth gritted, eyes screwed shut. It wasn't about the intensity of being penetrated, because the guy knew how to do that; it was something else, something psychological.

Slater closed his eyes and eventually came, collapsing on top of Rahim, and then, shifting down the bed, took Rahim into his mouth.

"It's for you," Rahim said, his tone sharp. "All for you."

Slater reached up and put his hand over Rahim's mouth, firmly grasping his face. That seemed to speed things up, and it took him only a minute more to come, in that moment grabbing Slater's hair and pulling him off, then meeting his mouth, finally flopping on his back.

Stretching out beside him, Slater covered his eyes with his arm. Rahim rolled on his side, composure restored, and after a while started tracing gentle figure eights on Slater's chest with a fingertip. It was hypnotic, sending Slater close to sleep, and he started when Rahim spoke.

"Did you go to school to learn to do what you do?"

"You mean the insurance field?" Slater asked, briefly lifting his arm to peer at him.

"I mean the hard-ass stuff. Interrogations,

and telling Gwen you'd burn her to the ground."

Interesting that the two of them were comparing notes, Slater thought. He'd had that conversation with her just this afternoon.

"My job is the kind of thing you have to learn by doing it," Slater said. "I did a community college program, but it was in horticulture."

"That explains a lot."

"Like what?" Slater demanded, lifting his arm to look at him again.

"You dress like a gardener."

"Fuck you—you dress like an outlet mall exploded."

Rahim chuckled. "Touché." After a minute, he asked, "Did you do sports in college?"

"I wrestled, but that was back in middle school."

"I could see that. You seem to know how to manhandle people." He shifted position, resting his palm on Slater's belly. "I played football."

"Seriously?" Slater said. "You seem too light. Football guys are thick and dumb."

"Not all of them. Some of the positions are about agility, not brawn."

"I do appreciate the cute little outfits. I couldn't play, though—I'd be too distracted by all that Spandex-clad man flesh."

"You have a one-track mind," Rahim said flatly.

"You can't tell me you think football's not supposed to be erotic."

"There's more to it. Sportsmanship, competition, the thrill of victory."

"Sportsmanship sounds useless. But you can fuck sportsmen."

Rahim scoffed. "If you were out there, instead of 'football,' they'd have to call it 'Slater tries to fuck twenty-one guys.'"

"Now, that, I'd pay to watch."

Rahim was quiet for a while, then said, "Uniforms."

"What?"

"We wore uniforms, not cute little outfits."

Slater chuckled. "Of course you did."

"Are you going to sleep over?"

"I have to go," Slater said, turning toward him and caressing his cheek.

Rahim rolled out of bed and went to the bathroom. Once the shower started, Slater quickly got up and went to the kitchen, grabbing Rahim's cell phone and typing the code to unlock it. On his own phone he found the software he needed, and held them back-to-back to transfer it, then spent a minute installing it. Setting Rahim's down again and walking back to the bedroom, he checked the tracking app on his own phone. There it was, a green dot on the map, showing him exactly where Rahim's phone was.

The shower was still running, and Slater got dressed, pulling on his jeans and his boots, then let himself out the front door. The last pinky-orange traces of the sun's descent were fading on the western horizon as he accelerated onto the freeway.

ear home, cruising on surface streets, his phone rang, the caller identified as "unknown," but the number was in area code 562—Downey. Slater picked up.

"Hello, Mr. Ibáñez. It's Derek Laird." His voice was deep, and it was a flawed connection, echoey, like Laird was in a small room, or using a cheap phone.

"Finally," Slater said. "You need to meet me."

"Can't we handle things this way? We're talking—what more do you need? I'm very fragile right now. Definitely not up for a meeting."

"Where are you?" Slater demanded. "You haven't been at the apartment you listed as your residence on the claim."

Laird paused before he spoke. "I'm staying

with a friend. I go to my apartment sometimes."

"You need to meet me. Tomorrow morning."

"I can't do that, Mr. Ibáñez. I'm just not up to it. I'll call you again in a day or two."

The line went dead as Slater pulled into his alley and waited for the garage door to roll up. Once he'd parked, he flipped open his satchel and checked the phone number Laird had given on his claim forms against the one he'd just called from; they matched.

Laird had another thing coming if he thought he could brush Slater off with a phone call. But that was for tomorrow, he thought, heading up the stairs, shifting focus to what was waiting for him. Loyal and constant, a stiff drink had nothing to hide, no reason to lie to him.

Ditching his satchel by the door, he found the bourbon in the cupboard, a lone bottle with an inch missing. That was weird, as there had been two bottles yesterday. Looking in the trash, sure enough, there was an empty.

Maybe he really was drinking a lot, as Doris had intimated, and as Conrad never hesitated to point out. He could quit when he needed to, he knew that much. Luckily he didn't need to. Were the two of them conspiring on this? It was nobody's freaking business but his own. And what had he said to Doris in that blackout phone conversation? That was the only part that was really worrying. Filling a tumbler, he took a big slurp, then refilled it and dropped in an ice cube.

On *Sasquatch Search* tonight they were in a lab, in Seattle, the narrator's voice calmly explaining the strands of hair they'd recovered, caught in the bark of a tree. Now it was under the microscope. Could it have anything to do with the strange cries in the night heard by hikers in that area?

Maybe Slater should get out of town for a while, somewhere like that, into the forest, out of this sprawling cesspool. He smiled to himself, and took another deep drink. Who was he kidding? He wouldn't know the first thing about how to function away from these gritty streets.

———•———

This was not going to be a good morning, he knew, waking with his head throbbing. Forcing himself up, he went to the bathroom and shook some ibuprofen into his mouth, then to the kitchen, where he ate some olives. In the cupboard he found a stray vegan Pop-Tart, and ate that while the microwave was heating up a mug of water. Dumping some coffee crystals into it, he swirled the murky tepid mess around with a spoon and took the mug to his recliner, where he sat for a minute, taking deep, slow breaths.

Sipping the pseudo-coffee, focusing on deepening his breathing, he started to feel better, and went back to the bedroom to retrieve his phone. Standing up made his head pound again, and he sank into the recliner when he got back, slow-breathing through his nose.

Conrad was home, the moron, way out in the Valley. Such a lazy ass. The tracker on Rahim's phone was working too, and the map showed him somewhere out east, along the 60. Zooming in, Slater saw that he was at a hospital. That didn't seem suspicious, or even revealing; it had to be work-related. He killed the screen and sat for a few more minutes, willing his head to stop throbbing, then got up and got dressed.

Down in his garage he opened his armored cabinet and checked that the devices he needed were charged, then put them into his satchel. Climbing into the Thunderbird, he backed into the alley and headed toward Ganesh. Slater parked in the lot, near the driveway to the street, and admired the trio of fan palms as he walked toward Ganesh's building. A black beamer drove past him, pulling up near the doors. Rahim climbed out and waited for Slater as he strode up.

"You must love it here," he said.

"I'm not here for you," Slater said. "I need to talk to Dave."

"About Derek Laird? What's going on?"

"Technically none of your damn business." Slater held his gaze. "I had fun last night."

Rahim just grinned and went inside.

When they walked into the lobby, the receptionist ignored Rahim but glared at Slater. Clearly she thought he'd been snooping in Gwen's office yesterday. Ignoring her call to "Wait a minute," he walked into the hallway that led to Dave's office.

Reclining in his chair with his feet on his desk, Dave looked up when he walked in, not rising, but setting aside the tablet he was holding.

"The insurance man," Dave said genially. "Still poking around, I see."

"I'm having trouble getting hold of your accountant," Slater said.

Dave waved him to a chair. "Laird? Have you tried going to his home? If he's disabled, I'd think that's where he'd be."

Freaking technical people, Slater thought, but swallowed his ire. "That's some clear and rational reasoning, Dave. I've been there repeatedly. If I can't talk to him, I'm going to have to stop his payouts."

Dave looked to the doorway, where Gwen had appeared. That receptionist must have alerted her to Slater's arrival.

"Are you talking about Derek?" she asked. "I asked him to phone you last night."

"He did, but that's not good enough," Slater said, eyeing her.

Dave swung his feet off his desk and sat

forward. "What do we do here, Gwen? You always handle this kind of stuff."

She sat in the chair next to Slater's, as though she'd been invited, looking thoughtful.

"I know he's a mess," she said, "but if he won't cooperate with you, maybe your company shouldn't be paying him. I could understand if Cudahy Mutual decided to void his coverage."

Slater watched her. She was trying to project sincerity, her dramatically made-up eyes wide. When people advised him to walk away, it usually meant there was something worth digging for.

"The thing is," Slater said, "the company is already paying him, and they're paying me. I'm not just going to drop it."

Gwen's brow furrowed in concern.

"He's a damn fool if he can't even do a two-minute interview," Dave said. "I don't care how shy he is, or how broken he is. I paid him plenty over the years. I can't imagine he really needs disability checks."

"Again, he's already accepting payment," Slater said.

"So what are you going to do—sue him to recoup the money?" Dave said. "It can't be that much. Sometimes it's better just to wash your hands. Save all those lawyers' fees."

"That's up to your company, of course," Gwen said, eyeing Slater. "He doesn't work here anymore, and we can't compel Derek to do anything."

"OK," Slater said evenly, looking from her to Dave, then rising and walking out.

Gwen caught up to him in the hallway, half-way back to the lobby, in front of the windows onto the workshop. Slater stopped and turned when she called "Ibáñez."

"Were you in my office yesterday after I left?" she asked.

"I'm curious why you'd bring that up here, but not in front of the boss."

She frowned. "He's got enough to worry about. I'm not going to burden him with this."

"And yet you're willing to hurl the accusation at me."

"What were you doing in my office?" she demanded.

"It says a lot, don't you think, that you have secrets from Dave? What else are you hiding?"

Turning away and walking through the lobby, he caught the receptionist's gaze, pointing two fingers at his own eyes, then jabbing his index finger at her: *I'm watching you.* It had the desired effect—she recoiled visibly.

Just outside, pulled up to the block stenciled THE BOSS, was a late-1980s plum-colored Eldorado. That had to be Dave's car. Why hadn't it been here before? No way was that a factory paint job, he thought, and it wasn't restored either, so someone had been driving it all these years. Dave must have done a lot of acid back in the day. Why else would anyone paint a car that color?

Snapping a quick photo of the Eldorado's rear plate, Slater stepped between it and Gwen's new white Benz and squatted down, twisting his satchel around and pulling out the tracking devices. Switching one of them on, he reached inside the wheel well of the Eldorado and found a spot where the tracker's magnetic base attached itself with a satisfying *click*. It took a little longer up under Gwen's Benz—newer cars had a lot less steel for the magnets to adhere to—but eventually he found a place for it. Rising, he scanned the parking lot, confirming that he hadn't been observed, and walked back to the Thunderbird. With eyes on both of them now, and on Rahim, maybe one of them would lead him to Derek Laird.

The trackers were Russian, and cleverly designed—they weren't as accurate as the software Slater had buried on Rahim's cell phone, because they didn't use GPS, instead sensing Wi-Fi signals. That meant they didn't work at all out of town, but in the city, Wi-Fi was ubiquitous, and the big tech companies knew the precise location of every Wi-Fi access point, hidden or locked or otherwise, happily sharing that information with anyone who cared to query their databases. It also meant the trackers could operate on low power, with a battery that would last for several days, and they didn't need an antenna or a view of the sky.

Slater drove downtown and parked, waving to the attendant as he headed across to his building, then checked his phone when it buzzed. It was a text from Miguel at the Baltimore:

> I just got interviewed on channel 6. You should check it out.

Riding the elevator up to his office, he'd barely put his phone away when it rang. He picked up when he saw that it was Rahim.

"I wanted to invite you to a house party tomorrow night," he said.

Slater sighed, wishing he'd never slept with him. It was impossible to sort out whether the guy's interest in Slater was personal and romantic, or something to do with Derek Laird.

"Is this something that came up since I saw you this morning?" Slater asked.

"I just forgot to mention it. You were being kind of prickly."

Twisting his key in the door to the office, he pushed his way inside, cradling the phone to his ear.

"Are you sure you want to see me again?" Slater said. "I'm not who you think I am."

"It's just a party. Come on, it's Saturday night."

"Why not? I'll see you then," Slater said, and ended the call.

Max stepped out of his office and stood in Slater's doorway. Today he'd swapped the seersucker for a dark-blue paisley jacket and a black shirt.

"Going on a second date?" Max said. "That must be a record for you."

"He's part of my insurance case," Slater said, setting his satchel on his desk.

"What happened to keeping your dick out of your cases?"

Slater wanted to punch that louche smile off his face, calling out Slater's hypocrisy, but he needed to work with this guy. Still, his rage must have shown in his expression.

"What?" Max demanded.

"That's such a good idea," he said flatly. "I wish I'd remembered that before I slept with him."

Max chuckled. "They're your rules, not mine."

"Can you help me out tonight? I need to do a site reconnaissance."

"Absolutely—where are we going?"

"South Gate," Slater said, and explained what he'd seen at Laird's oddly down-market and seemingly abandoned apartment, his chat with the manager, and the results of the video surveillance.

"If his girlfriend let herself in there, why not just ask her?" Max said.

"I don't think she's his girlfriend. I know she's smart, and she's definitely up to something with him, but they don't need to know what I know."

"I get it," Max said, nodding. "Tread carefully, and go in with two sets of eyes. What time do you want to do this?"

"Not too late. Let's meet here at eleven."

"Right—you've got your date."

"That's tomorrow," Slater said irritably.

"You know, you should go down to the flower market and take him one of those wrist corsages. They're so much easier to wear than the ones you pin on." Max tapped his lapel.

"At least my dates aren't inflatable."

"Oh," Max cried, arching his back. "I actually do pretty well with women."

"Tucking singles into a dancer's G-string isn't a date, Max."

Max laughed and went back to his office, calling good-bye as he left shortly after. Slater settled in at his desk. A search for Laird's phone number turned up nothing, until he compared it to numbers controlled by spoofing services, like the one he and Max used sometimes on outgoing calls. And there it was—Laird's was part of a block of numbers owned by a spoofing company. It was a legitimate provider, renting numbers to doctors, shelters, and others who had valid reasons to conceal their identity or a personal number, rather than one that enabled telemarketing scams, but still—why would an accountant need a fake phone number?

Miguel's text, he remembered. Channel 6. Pulling up the TV station's website, he scrolled through the news articles, and soon found what had to be the headline for the story Miguel was talking about: "Lipo Doc Dumps Ailing Patient." Slater clicked on the video, which began with a glamorously coiffed twenty-something reporter in a tight sleeveless top, gripping a foam-headed microphone with a big yellow 6 on it and intently eyeing the camera. She was standing in front of a familiar building—the Samaritan hospital, Slater realized, right near his apartment.

"Shocking unethical medical practices have come to light tonight," she said, despite the fact that it was clearly broad daylight behind her, "involving a physician who's already on the DA's radar for what investigators have called excessive prescription of opioids. Dr. Lynn Cheung runs a liposuction clinic in Pico Rivera."

Wrong, Slater thought, but close. It was in Downey; he'd been there.

"Glenda Cutler was treated last Sunday," the reporter continued, her expression earnest, "and then dumped in a guest room at the Baltimore Hotel in downtown Los Angeles, where she developed a nasty infection. Doctors here say that if she'd waited much longer, that infection"—she paused for effect—"would have cost her life."

The video cut to a woman propped up in a hospital bed, machines and wires all around, her red hair bundled neatly at one shoulder. Cutler, he realized. She looked a lot better than when Slater had talked to her. "It was just a little liposuction," she said. "I had no idea my life was at risk. I'm truly grateful to the man who called in the cavalry. His name is Miguel, and he's a concierge at the Baltimore."

Talking over a clip that slowly panned the hotel's facade, the reporter said, "We tracked down Miguel Hernández, who didn't remember the intervention at first. He says it's all part of the job."

The image cut to Miguel, looking sweaty and uncomfortable, squinting at the camera lights and standing in front of a purpose-built press-conference backdrop, white with a not-subtle repeating pattern of the hotel's logo printed on it.

"I was concerned for her well-being," Miguel said. "I'm no doctor, but I knew from talking to her that she had a fever, and her incisions were infected. I'm just glad she's going to be all right."

Slater grinned, watching him squirm. Cutler had identified Miguel by the nametag on the jacket Slater had worn that day, and now Miguel had to go with her version of the story. She might not have seen the real Miguel yet, but even if she had, she'd been feverish when Slater visited her, and one brown guy was probably indistinguishable from the next.

The video cut back to the live shot outside the hospital. "LA police are handling the case," the reporter explained, "and tell us the investigation is ongoing. For now, Miguel Hernández can be proud tonight that his concierge services extend"—she paused—"to saving a life. Back to you in the studio."

Slater thumb-typed a text to Miguel:

> You're very photogenic on video. I'm so glad you stepped up to help that woman. If there's reward money, I want half.

He should probably be grateful, he knew, that Miguel had kept Slater's name out of it. That kind of attention only made his job harder.

Turning back to his computer, he checked on the vehicle trackers he'd placed today. Both of them were regularly connecting to the cell network, as they were supposed to, and submitting location data. The map showed two green circles, indicating a general location rather than a precise point. The circles overlapped each other around Ganesh's building in Downey. Slater set the app to alert him when they started to move.

Pulling up the app connected to Rahim's

phone, the dot showed that he was in Downey too, but not at Ganesh. When he looked closer, it was a strip mall, and the dot was in front of a building at one end of it, labeled DOWNEY ORANGE GROWERS BANK. Then it started to move, out onto the boulevard, and he watched as the dot slowly drifted to the freeway and picked up speed, heading north.

Slater got up and stuffed his phone in his pants, pulling his satchel over his shoulder. Hopefully he could catch up.

When he climbed into his car, he checked the app again. Rahim was passing downtown on the 110, moving surprisingly quickly on that perpetually congested artery. The green dot exited as he watched, crawling eastbound along the ramp onto Sixth Street and into the Financial District, stopping a few blocks later, where the dot turned gray, its location no longer certain. Slater zoomed in. The software had lost track of him at the entrance to a parking garage under an office tower. That's where Rahim was, and it was close—just a couple of minutes' drive.

Slater started the engine and drove up to the Financial District, passing the entrance to the lot Rahim had taken and scanning for street parking. A minute later he found a meter, climbed out and fed it a credit card, then walked back toward the building, looking at his phone for the reappearance of Rahim's green dot, trying not to collide with other pedestrians on the busy sidewalk.

The dot was visible again: Rahim was in another freaking bank, right next to where he'd parked, the Commerce and Credit Development Bank. Why had Slater heard of that? It was too much work to jostle with the crowds of office workers while he was trying to focus on the little screen, so he stepped into the sidewalk patio of a coffeehouse, sitting at an open table.

A quick Web search reminded him what he'd heard about the bank. Owned by oligarchs from the Balkans, it had been accused of enabling money laundering, and was under investigation by regulators in Florida. What business would Rahim have in a place like that?

He decided to walk in and see. If Rahim spotted him, he'd play it off as a chance meeting. The bank was on the ground floor of an office building, and Slater checked for the green dot again as he crossed the lobby. It had moved, farther back now, in a space that was labeled PUB AND GRILL. But the back wall of the lobby was just a row of elevators, no restaurant in sight.

Slater approached a security guard. "How do I get into the restaurant?"

The guy frowned. "There's nothing like that here."

Walking toward the bank, which was clearly

marked at one side of the space, Slater stepped inside. There was no armed guard, like at most banks, just a woman at a long glass desk facing the door. Giving Slater the once-over, she rose, preparing to come over to talk to him. She looked expensive—this was a place for wealthy people and private consultations, not a regular bank with tellers and cubicles. Clearly he couldn't walk around snooping, even if Rahim was here. Before the woman could walk over, he went back into the lobby.

The accuracy of the location tracker was imperfect, he knew, especially indoors, where it relied on Wi-Fi. Glancing around, he compared the space to the map on his phone. The restaurant with the dot in it was on the ground floor, so that wasn't the issue. Then he saw that it wasn't even in this building—it was in the neighboring structure, abutting this one back-to-back. There was no direct access. He'd have to go out to the street and around.

Rahim had parked right here, not at the building on the next street, he thought as he walked, so maybe he had done a quick errand at that bank. After turning both street corners, he entered the ground floor of another office tower. This place was older, airier, with white tile. And there was the restaurant, right at the back, its interior warmly lit.

No one was at the front desk, and Slater stepped inside and looked around, soon spotting Rahim. He was sitting on a barstool, next to a blond in a blue summer suit. They were facing each other, their knees almost touching. Blondie laughed heartily, touching Rahim's forearm. That didn't look like a business meeting.

Rahim glanced in Slater's direction, recognition registering in his expression. He shot Slater a quizzical look. Slater walked over and stood next to them, hands on hips, and had a look at the blond. The guy was hot, of course. How could this play out any other way?

"What are you doing here?" Rahim said, a stupid grin on his face.

"Cudahy Mutual's offices are in the next block," Slater said, and jutting his chin at the blond, "Who's your boyfriend?"

"He's not my boyfriend. Mike, this is Slater."

"Hey," Mike said, his tone uncertain.

"You forgot to cut the price tag off your suit," Slater said, pointing to Mike's cuff.

Mike didn't look, but his eyes narrowed.

Slater turned to Rahim. "Shouldn't you be at work?"

"I am at work. We're talking business."

"And sharing a plate of fries," Slater said. "That seems pretty intimate. At least you each got your own beer." Looking at Mike, he said, "Not afraid of cooties, Mike? Or are you already past that point?"

Mike looked at Rahim. "I'm going to the head," he said, and slid off the stool, walking away.

"He seems kind of crass," Slater said, watching him go. "Does he think he's on a frigate, or at a Parisian *vespasienne*?"

"You're the one who's crass," Rahim said intently. "You and I aren't together, Slater. Why are you acting like this?"

"It's nothing to do with me," he said sharply. "You're the one sharing french fries with the peroxide job. He seems kind of standoffish, doesn't he? That type is really boring in the sack. They make you do all the work."

Rahim stared at him. "You are such a weirdo. I find you so compelling."

"You want weird, chum, just look a little closer at your boyfriend. I wouldn't be surprised if he was a Klansman."

Rahim scoffed. "He's not my boyfriend."

"I'd better go, before Prince Charming returns. I guess I missed the opportunity for a men's room beatdown."

"Why would you say something like that?" he demanded.

Slater shrugged. "Men's rooms are great for fighting—there are never any surveillance cameras."

Rahim rubbed his forehead and sighed. "Are we still on for tomorrow?"

"Will Blondie be there?"

"Probably not."

"I'll see you then," Slater said, and walked out. On his left he saw Mike exiting the men's room, but ignored him, heading into the lobby.

"Hey," said a sharp voice behind him.

Slater turned to find Mike, glaring at him, fists balled at his sides. Slater instantly recognized the stance—the slight curve to his back, the elbows turned out to the optimal degree, his ears floating away from his shoulders. This guy knew how to use those fists.

"Do you need help with something?" Slater asked. "It looked like you were doing fine in there—you had Rahim eating out of the palm of your hand."

"What is your problem with me?" Mike demanded.

"It's nothing personal. I just have an aversion to"—he looked him up and down pointedly—"cheap suits."

Before he could react, Mike's arm flew out, lightning fast, as he punched Slater in the mouth.

Slater touched his lip, glaring at him. "What was that for?"

"I had this tailor-made in Singapore. It was not cheap."

"Fine. It brings out your eyes." Glancing around the lobby, Slater said, "Put your paws down, bub. There's no cause for a brawl here. We'll both get popped."

Mike dropped his hands to his sides, breathing heavily. "I don't know what you think is going on, but I'm not with Rahim. He sells equipment to my business."

"Where did you learn to move like that?" Slater asked. "Such celerity." It had been a remarkable blow, surgically precise, demanding his attention without doing any damage.

"I boxed in college."

"Of course you did. Ivy League, I suppose."

Mike grinned. "Close."

"You shouldn't go around punching people. You might get hurt."

"You shouldn't go around making assumptions about people," Mike said. "Rahim's all yours, if that's what this is about."

Slater held up both hands. "Nothing to do with me," he said, and turned to walk out to the sidewalk and back to his car.

Rahim was right, he knew—Slater was being a dick, and Mike was justified in taking offense. "Listen and repeat," a shrink had once told him. Before he reacted, she wanted him to listen to what he wanted to say in his own head and repeat it as if someone else were saying it. It took a lot of work, trying to do that in the moment, the effort of pausing and thinking it through, so Slater usually just spoke, and that meant he was usually a dick.

Why would Rahim invite him over for sex, twice, and then sit there drinking beer with a goddamn textbook pretty boy? How was that in any way not infuriating? Maybe he should have punched back. But the guy was skilled, and Slater might not have won that fight. You had to know when to walk away.

SEVEN

Friday traffic was heavy, and it took a while to get back to his own neighborhood, even though it was nearby, just across the chasm of the 110. Along the way he nosed the Thunderbird into the parking lot of a supermarket. He hated these places, hated going into them, but like sitting in traffic, they were inevitable.

Spending just enough time to get a couple of basics and three fifths of bourbon, Slater loaded everything on the belt at the checkout. The checker was a Latin kid with nattily coiffed hair, grinning as he dragged Slater's purchases across the scanner.

"Rye bread, peanut butter, and booze—somebody's got a fun night planned," he said.

Slater handed him a sheaf of bills and looked

toward the ceiling, spotting several lenses trained on the registers. "Lots of cameras in here, huh."

"What, are you camera-shy?" the kid asked, handing him his change and then deftly loading the bottles into a shopping bag.

"No, but it means it's not worth it for me to dick-punch you."

His eyebrows shot up. "Why would you do that?"

"The question is, why wouldn't I do that? It's called self-control. I'm able to resist the strong desire to punch you, and there's some degree of satisfaction in that. You should try it: resist saying every stupid fucking thing that pops into your head."

Scooping up his bags, Slater walked out to the parking lot.

Once he was home and had carried the bags upstairs, he ate a piece of rye bread with nothing on it, then tossed the rest of the loaf in the refrigerator. He should probably get a toaster, he thought, and sat in the recliner, opening the hookup app. Rahim had lied to him, sloppily and repeatedly, but Slater had no perspective on the guy, no objectivity. One way to stop thinking about him was to sleep with someone else. It was early to be looking for a hookup, but the advantage to early guys was that more of them were likely to be sober.

After a few minutes of swiping through

images of body parts and head shots, he found a dark-haired guy with a nice smile and nice pecs, and not very far away. Slater texted him:

I want to fuck you. My place. No drugs.

His reply came momentarily:

I am sober as a judge. Text me your address.

After he'd sent it, Slater stowed the new bottles of bourbon in the kitchen cupboard, then hid his satchel behind the sofa. His phone dinged, and when he pulled it out to look, he saw that Gwen's car was moving. He wasn't going to run surveillance on her tonight, but at least he knew the tracker was working.

There was a knock at the door, and Slater pulled it open to find the guy from the app. In person he looked older, maybe in his late forties, but he was still hot.

"You look great," the guy said, beaming and stepping inside, and then, "Whoa—what a dive."

"Thank you," Slater said. "Are you actually a judge?"

He frowned. "What?"

"The app said you were eight hundred yards away, which is exactly the distance from here to that courthouse on Sixth. Plus you texted that you were sober as a judge."

"It's kind of scary that you put all that together. I'm no judge. One day, maybe—I'm in that field."

"What's your name?"

"How about Mark?"

"Whatever you say," Slater said, and stepped toward him. More like a Marcos, he thought, with a Latin vibe, but he didn't say that; Slater hated when people did that to him, making assumptions about his ethnicity. "So what do you want to do, Mark?"

Mark frowned. "I thought you said you wanted to fuck me."

Slater nodded. "I do," he said, and led him to his bedroom, pulling him down onto the futon. Mark wasn't hesitant at all, undressing while he met Slater's mouth with his own. He moved deliberately, like he was well practiced, and took charge of pulling off Slater's clothes. Once they were both naked, he straddled Slater, groping him until he was hard and then deftly rolling a condom on him, without even looking. Sliding down onto Slater's cock, the guy did most of the work, and came with Slater inside him. That didn't happen very often. Watching him was such a turn-on, and Slater soon came too.

Mark climbed off and lay down beside him, draping an arm across Slater's still heaving chest.

"You do this a lot?" Slater asked.

"Why do you say that?"

"You seem to know what you're doing. Efficient, I'd say."

"Well, I know what I want."

"That works for me," Slater said, covering his eyes with the crook of his arm.

———◆———

The room was dark when he woke to the feeling of a warm body climbing into bed beside him.

"Rahim?"

"Who's Rahim?" the guy asked.

Slater willed himself awake, waited for his mind to get clearer.

"I'm half asleep," he said finally. "What was your name again?"

"I think I said Mark."

Slater scoffed. "If you can't even remember, why would it matter what I called you?"

"Did you know your stove doesn't work?" Mark said, ignoring the question. "There's no gas coming out of any of the burners."

"I didn't know that. I never use it." Slater shifted position. "What were you trying to cook?"

"I wanted to unclog my vape pen. The cannabis oil sometimes dries up where the hole is, but you can melt it again with a little heat."

"Is everyone in this town a freaking doper?" Slater demanded.

"It's just a little pot. I'm not even smoking up your house—it's vapor. Completely harmless."

"I have to work tonight," Slater said, sitting up. "You have to leave."

"Yeah, that happens a lot with you early birds," he said, and got up, clicking the light on.

Slater watched him getting dressed.

"Can I get your number?" Mark asked, sitting on the edge of the bed to tie his shoes. "I work in your neighborhood."

"Look for me on the app," Slater said, and swung his feet to the floor, rubbing his eyes.

Digging through his closet, he found a clean black shirt, and as he was buttoning it, he heard Mark leave. In the kitchen, standing at the counter, he ate another piece of dry rye bread and checked his phone for his various trackers.

Gwen was in the Arts District, the wide green circle centered on Mateo Street, where her apartment was. More interesting, Rahim was in the same area, his green dot within the radius of her circle. Slater didn't even bother to double-check her address. There were restaurants galore in that part of town, but this was too much to be a coincidence—Rahim was at Gwen's place. Were they just friends because they worked together, or was something else going on?

Dave's car was in the general vicinity of his own house in Downey, which seemed boring, to be sitting at home on Friday night. There was a chance the Eldorado wasn't the car he drove every day, as Slater had been to Ganesh twice before he noticed it parked there. But for now that was all he had on the guy.

Dick-smack Conrad was in Studio City. What the hell was he doing there? Zooming in on the dot on the map, Slater realized he knew the place: a dance bar on Ventura Boulevard that played country music on weekends. Freaking idiot. Why was Doris so enamored with a guy who had nothing better to do than shake his butt in a bar full of sweaty guys? Dancing, drinking, flirting, with that perfect smile, sweat glistening in his hair, picking up some hot guy, kissing him in the car before they drove home. Slater killed the app, frustrated at the thought.

He pulled on his satchel and headed down to his garage, but halfway there he turned around and trotted back up, remembering that he wanted to take his laptop, so he could see what the smoke-detector camera had picked up at Laird's door.

Max's car, a matte-gray Challenger with dark tinted windows, was already in the parking lot when he got downtown, and when Slater walked into the office, he found Max crouched in front of the safe, setting his weapon and its holster inside, his jacket draped on Slater's desk beside their illicit Russian lock-breaking gear.

Rather than old-school deadbolt-picking tools, it consisted of a probe with a length of wire that connected to an app on their phones, accompanied by a thick zippered binder with hundreds of master keys in it. When the probe was inserted into a regular lock, it usually spat out the number of a key. It only worked on standard hardware-store locks, but that's what most doors had, and anyone who bothered to upgrade to high-security locks would also have other more sophisticated measures in place to prevent break-ins—Slater wouldn't even try to get through those.

Max stood up and greeted him, reaching for his jacket.

"You look naked without your weapon," Slater said.

"We're not going to get caught, but if we do, I want to be unarmed."

"No ifs. We're not going to get caught."

"I pulled out the key set and the lock reader," Max said. "Do we need anything else?"

"The socket cameras."

Max stooped and pulled them out of the safe, tossing them onto Slater's desk.

"And ball caps. There's an overhead camera at the entrance to the building, but none in the corridor or at the apartment door."

Slater packed the key case and the tech gear into his satchel, then stepped out to the tiny front office, where a coat rack held a lone black umbrella of uncertain provenance and two blue ball caps. The woman who'd rented them their office furniture had thrown in the coat rack as part of the deal. "Your clients might wear hats, and overcoats," she'd said, and even though that sounded far-fetched in a subtropical city, they'd let her deliver it along with the desks and chairs.

Stuffing the ball caps into his bag, Slater pulled open the outer door.

"Want me to drive?" Max asked, following him into the hall.

"You know it," he said, and once they were across the street, climbed into the passenger seat of the Challenger, setting the heavy bag on the floor under his knees.

The map on his phone advised them to take the freeway, and Slater gave Max directions once they were on surface streets in South Gate. Max parked half a block away and killed the engine.

"I'll go alone to read the lock," Slater said, pulling the probe out of his satchel. "I don't want to be hunting through the key case there."

Max muttered assent, and Slater plugged the probe into his phone and started the app. The screen went black, displaying only the Cyrillic word "готов," whatever that meant, inside a circle.

Pulling on one of the ball caps and adjusting it low over his brow, he climbed out and walked to Laird's door, keeping his head down as he passed the mailboxes and the security camera.

Banging on Laird's door, he listened, but there was no movement inside. Slater stood close and slid the probe into the lock, glancing back toward the street and then watching the screen on his phone. It went red and said "ошибка." He didn't know the word, but he knew that it meant it wasn't working. Taking a breath to steady himself, he pulled the probe out slightly, lifting it a little, and almost instantly the screen went green and displayed a lone number: 426.

Success. He couldn't help but smile as he pocketed the probe and his phone, then paused to pull down his smoke-detector camera from the crossbeam in the corridor before returning to Max's car, glancing furtively over his shoulder to make sure he was alone.

"Did it work?" Max asked as he climbed in. He was already wearing his ball cap, anticipating the excursion.

"It came up with just one option."

"Right on."

"You find the key," Slater said, reciting the number and heaving the heavy case out of his bag, handing it to Max. "I want to check the surveillance footage."

With a fingernail he pried the memory card out of the smoke-detector camera, then pulled open his laptop, sliding the card into it. Several moth flights had been dutifully recorded, but no human visitors had come to Laird's door.

Slater folded the computer closed and took the key case back, setting it on the floor, then dug two pairs of black latex gloves out of his bag, handing a pair to Max. When they'd both pulled them on, they climbed out of the Challenger and walked toward Laird's building, heads down. As they approached the mailboxes, Slater reached into his satchel and flipped the heavy switch on the frequency jammer, illuminating a very bright blue indicator light on the device's dull metal housing. More sketchy Russian tech, it interfered with cellular and Wi-Fi signals in the area, with the goal of disrupting any wireless alarm system or video camera. It was a drastic measure, and extremely illegal, but if they kept it to a brief interval, the neighbors would be back online before they suspected anything more than fleeting Internet provider incompetence.

Gesturing to Laird's door, Slater checked the time on his phone as Max twisted the key in the lock, pushing his way in. Slater closed the door gently behind them.

Max flipped on the lights and scanned the room. "No alarm panel," he said quietly.

Slater went through the apartment as quickly as he could. It was a basic, tired place, with Berber carpet and vertical blinds, presenting the same cheap vibe as the building did on the outside. In the main room were a sofa, a lounge chair, and a couple of tables. A brass model of the Eiffel Tower sat on the coffee table, along with a Magic 8-Ball. Slater picked it up and turned it over, reading the message that came up in the little window: BETTER NOT TELL YOU NOW.

Setting it down again, he examined the framed photos on the end table—one of a man and woman and three kids, the other of an elderly couple. Both were portraits, the subjects smiling. None of them were Derek Laird, and they didn't look like him, necessarily, but they could be relatives. Pulling out his phone, he snapped a quick photo of each.

In the lone bedroom, where the bed was neatly made, sliding open the closet, he found shirts and suits. Flicking on the light in the bathroom revealed towels, bottled toiletries, a toothbrush beside the basin. Laird had been living here, it seemed, even if he hadn't been around lately.

As Slater stepped back into the living room, he found Max holding a round white desk clock, peering intently at it.

"How many clocks do you have in your place?" Max asked.

"Zero. There's a clock on my phone."

"Exactly. Nobody needs these nowadays. It's a camera. It was sitting on that end table beside the sofa, pointed at the front door."

"Broadcasting?"

"I don't think so," Max said. "It's got a memory card in it."

"Can you disable it?"

"It has a power switch, but shouldn't we just take the whole thing?"

"Then you're tipping off Laird, or whoever put it there, that someone came in, and knew what it was."

"I'll take the memory card. If it's not wireless, that should do it."

Slater looked at the fridge while Max messed with the clock camera. Taped on the front was the business card of a doctor, but not Lynn Cheung. He snapped a quick photo of it. Inside, the fridge was almost as barren as his own, with a jar of mayo, a bottle of ketchup, a quart of milk.

In the cupboard were a box of breakfast cereal and a package of cookies. The kitchen drawers revealed nothing but basic utensils, and sitting inverted on a towel beside the sink were two bowls, a glass, and a couple of spoons. The sink smelled sour, and Slater looked in the disposal, pushing aside the baffle with a latex-clad finger. The bottom was littered with bits of breakfast cereal.

"There's a make and model number in this thing," Max called. "Do you have your phone handy?"

Slater stepped over and photographed the label inside the clock's battery compartment. "Are there any others?"

"I'll keep looking," he said, and set the clock on the end table, adjusting the angle toward the front door.

Slater scanned the living room again. At the wall a desk had an unattached power cable draped over it, ready to plug into a laptop, along with a cheap printer, but there was no computer. The desk drawers were unlocked. In the bottom one was a set of hanging folders, labeled by month, although they didn't contain any files. If they were about Laird's work, it made sense the paper would have gone back to Ganesh.

The top drawer was shallower, and lying flat in it was a stack of thick blue-bound documents. Slater sat and pulled them out, flipping open the top one, then leafing through the others. They were tax returns, all of them for Derek Laird.

There wasn't enough time to read through them, but a figure on the first page of the latest return caught his eye. It listed Laird's gross income as seventy grand—far less than the seven figures Della had quoted. Hurriedly flipping through, his black latex–clad fingers sticking to the paper, he saw that Laird was deducting his home office, and a car, and property taxes paid to San Bernardino County. It must be a country house—the land description started with "four acres" and had latitude and longitude coordinates instead of an address, but in the CITY box, he'd typed "Big Bear, CA." Maybe it was a weekend place; there were lots of them up there. The snow would be gone by now—maybe it's where Laird was living.

Standing over the desk, he photographed the page with the property description, and the front page with the incongruous income figure.

"Four minutes," Max said, and he was right, it was a long time to be messing with people's phones and Internet connectivity.

"I'm ready," Slater said, and pulled the zip-top bag of socket cameras out of his satchel, finding the one that most closely matched the design of the apartment's electrical sockets. Kitchens usually had the sockets higher up than in other rooms, above the countertops, and Slater shifted the microwave over a few inches, exposing its plug, and pressed his camera into the open socket above it. Eyeballing it, the lens was pointed generally at the kitchen sink.

The camera was flat and made of the same beige plastic, designed to look like an open socket, the tiny lens concealed in one of the painted-on "holes." It drew power from the wall and connected to the cell network, alerting an app on Slater's phone whenever someone walked by. Even if Laird discovered it, the camera was pretty innocuous looking, hopefully easily mistaken for a childproof cap.

"You're just leaving the one?" Max asked.

"It should be enough. I just need to know whether Laird ever comes here." Slater made sure the camera was pressed in flush to the socket and then walked toward the front door.

"No other cameras," Max said quietly, following Slater into the corridor and then locking the door.

When they were out on the sidewalk, Slater switched off the jammer, extinguishing the brilliant blue indicator, intentionally designed to be so bright that it wouldn't inadvertently be forgotten.

"Hey," a woman's voice called from behind them.

"Keep walking," Slater said quietly, not looking back. He knew that voice: the manager of the building.

"Hey, did I talk to you a couple days ago?" she shouted.

Slater kept up a brisk pace, and Max stepped into the street behind the Challenger. She didn't follow them, and as soon as they'd climbed into the car, Max started the throaty engine and pulled away from the curb.

"Friend of yours?" Max asked.

"The manager. She definitely made me."

"Does she know your name?"

"Only my face. When I talked to her, I slipped her a twenty, so I don't think there's anything to worry about."

"She could have seen my license plate."

"Too far away. And even if she suspects we went inside, we didn't damage the lock, and we didn't take anything—no evidence."

Max parked again on a quiet street a few blocks away, and they peeled off their gloves. Slater took a deep breath to dispel the adrenaline.

"Can we check out the clock camera?" Max said. "It looks like basic hardware-store spy gear to me, but if it has internal memory, we should go back for it—we'll be recorded on it."

"We'd have to go later, after that woman is asleep," Slater muttered, and pulled out his phone, zooming in on the photo he'd taken of the device's label, then typing the model number into a Web search and reading through the results.

"You're right, it's consumer tech," he said finally. "It costs thirty bucks and you can buy it at the mall. Battery operated, video stored on a removable card. Taking out the card disables it."

"Excellent," Max said, and pulled away from the curb, heading toward the freeway.

Slater watched the dark city roll by. "It looks

like someone lives there, don't you think? I know Laird hasn't been home for three days, but Gwen stopped by yesterday morning. I wonder if she brought the clock camera to spy on him?"

"Wouldn't you notice if someone put a clock in your house?" Max said. "If she has a key, she must be sleeping with him."

"Maybe."

"Or maybe she copied his keys at some point, and he doesn't know she has access."

"She didn't knock before she went in yesterday, which means she knew he wasn't there."

Max scoffed. "Like I said, she's sleeping with him."

"Not necessarily. But it means she knows more about him than she wanted me to think."

"She's the DV, right? Maybe she choked him out too—permanently."

"Give me the card from the clock camera," Slater said, and Max reached inside his jacket pocket, keeping one hand on the steering wheel.

Slater turned on the dome light and opened his laptop, sliding the chip into it. There were just two files, and he clicked on the oldest one. A black-and-white fish-eye view of the room showed him and Max pushing in through the front door and surveying the apartment. There was no audio, but even with their ball caps on, from the camera's low angle, their faces were clearly recognizable. The other video was even more incriminating. Slater watched himself step into the frame. He glanced around, then picked up the Magic 8-Ball and inverted it, studying the bottom for a moment. Stepping closer to the camera, when he was examining the framed photos on the end table, he remembered, his face was distorted by the wide-angle lens, but it was still undeniably Slater, filling half the frame.

"The only recordings are you and me in there tonight," he said. "I'm so glad you caught this."

Max accelerated on the ramp, merging into the traffic on the 60. "I guess two heads are better than one."

Slater put away the laptop and looked at the tracking apps on his phone. Conrad was home already, probably with some twink he'd picked up in that bar, dressed like a freaking cowboy. There were no cowboys in the Valley, you trash bag, only suburban posers. Real cowboys don't wear leopard-print faux-fur cowboy hats. Swiping him away, he saw that Rahim was at his house, and Dave and Gwen's cars were home too.

"How does your day look tomorrow?" he asked Max.

"I'm open until eight."

"I've got trackers on two vehicles. I'm thinking these desk jockeys tend to cram a lot into their Saturdays, and I can only watch one at a time."

"I can follow one of them, sure."

"Gwen," Slater said. "White Mercedes convertible."

"Not an uncommon car in this town, but it'll be easy if I can track her on the map."

"I don't care if she's at home or at her company. You only have to go after her if she goes somewhere interesting. She knows me, but she's never seen you before—you can get close."

———◆———

Max dropped him at the office, where Slater unloaded the surveillance gear from his satchel, plugging in the frequency jammer and his smoke-detector camera to recharge. Lifting the heavy key case into the safe, he saw Max's weapon, dull and deadly, peeking out of its holster on a shelf inside. They really did trust each other—Max knew Slater would be opening the safe again tonight, but he drove off and left his heater here anyway.

Downstairs again, stepping out onto the dark deserted street, he looked around, scanning for observers. No need to worry about being seen now, he reminded himself. He wasn't doing anything he could get busted for.

Driving home, he knew what was waiting, a satisfyingly full bottle of bourbon. Once he'd dropped his satchel, he went into the kitchen and pulled it out, appreciating the delicious sound of the seal cracking as he twisted it open. Filling a tumbler, he paused to do a neck roll, then drank, the liquid burning his throat, warming his belly. He filled the glass again, then went to the sofa, feeling the amber glow starting to suffuse his entire being. Pulling off his boots and stretching out, he was too tired now even for bigfoot, instead listening only to the muted roar of the metropolis beyond his walls.

EIGHT

His head didn't hurt too badly when he woke up. He must have fallen asleep early, although he had no memory of climbing into bed. Waiting for a mug of water to heat up in the microwave, he ate a spoonful of peanut butter and then made cowboy coffee, guzzling it and grabbing a slice of rye bread to eat on the way down to the garage.

The streets were quiet on Saturday morning, and the drive to the office went fast. His phone buzzed as he was walking across the street from the parking lot, and he pulled it out to glance at it. Gwen's car was on the move.

A few of the sewing factories were open, but not on his floor, and once he was in the office, he checked all his trackers. The only one moving was Gwen. Max's keys rattled in the outer door, and soon he appeared, wearing his sharp gray grid-pattern suit with a navy tie.

"What have we got?" he asked.

"Gwen's on the move. Let me text you a photo of her tag," Slater said, tapping at his phone.

Max went behind Slater's desk and stooped at the safe door, dialing in the combination and retrieving his weapon.

"You said it was a white Benz?" he asked, in front of Slater's desk again, sliding off his jacket to strap on his holster.

"Convertible. Brand new. I know she's involved with Derek Laird, and with any luck she'll lead you to him."

"Do you have photos of these people?" Max said, shrugging his jacket back on.

"Right," Slater said, digging the case file out of his satchel, then handing Max the head shot of Gwen.

"She's pretty hot." Max studied the image for a minute.

"If you say so." Slater traded the photo for another sheet. "This is Laird."

"Got it," he said, handing it back.

"Let's get the tracker set up on your phone."

They spent a few minutes installing the software from the bright-yellow thumb drive that Slater kept in the safe, purchased from the

Russians along with the surveillance gear, and soon Max was looking at a map superimposed with the green circle indicating Gwen's location.

"It looks like she's on the 10 westbound," Max said, peering at the screen. "How long will the tracker last?"

"I put it on yesterday, so it should work until tomorrow sometime. It goes into low-power mode when the car is parked, and she hasn't moved around a lot, so maybe even longer."

"I'll go after her now," Max said. "We'll see whether she meets anyone interesting or not."

After Max was gone, Slater put his feet up on his desk and checked on Dave, but his vehicle hadn't moved. Conrad, however, was downtown. What the hell was he doing down here? Another clandestine outing with Doris? Slater zoomed in on the map. The dot was inside police headquarters. That was probably legit, he had to admit, as it was related to his job. At least he wasn't out blowing off steam, cruising guys in some pub, hooking up. Who was he sleeping with, anyway, the big dummy? It had to be someone. Maybe Doris would know, but no way was he going to ask her.

Absently looking at the tracker on Dave's Eldorado again, he swung his boots off his desk when he saw that it had moved. Maybe that was his everyday car. Rather than gliding along a smooth trajectory like the phone trackers, the ones on the cars worked differently, the location circle jumping from place to place. It seemed like Dave was getting on the freeway. Slater watched intently as he moved into the Arts District. Was he headed to Gwen's? Her Mercedes, and presumably Gwen herself, were long gone, headed west. But Dave kept moving through her neighborhood, stopping finally in Skid Row, right where it overlapped with the Fashion District. The circle stayed in the same spot but shrank, and then shrank again as the tracker sniffed out more Wi-Fi signals and the software gained confidence about its precise location. Dave had definitely parked the Eldorado, and it was just a few blocks from here—Slater could be there in minutes on foot.

Pocketing his phone, he went down to the street and walked up to Fifth, striding past the storefronts of the fashion industry, most of them closed today but some selling fabric and fittings, others retailing finished garments, hats, and wigs. He spotted Dave's car half a block before he got to it—that plum paint job was so distinct. It was odd to see the flashy Cadillac parked at a meter in a trash-strewn gutter. What was Dave doing around here? Heavy metal shutters covered most of the storefronts, but there was one place he might be, a newish multistory construction with SKID ROW RESIDENCES on the sign over the entrance.

That had to be it. Dave wasn't here to buy buttons or zippers or *quinceañera* dresses, but what would he be doing in a Skid Row housing complex? Looking the place over, it wasn't just residential, he realized, with a little library or bookshop visible through the windows on the ground floor.

The security guard nodded to him, unconcerned, as he walked in. At least Slater didn't look like a thief, or a drug dealer, or some other threat to the homeless who were sheltered here, but that wasn't really a mollifying thought; maybe the guy thought he lived here, or like Punch-face Rahim had said, maybe he looked like the gardener. The woman running the little shop, a head taller than Slater, shot him a gap-tooth smile. Slater nodded in greeting and went farther inside.

There seemed to be a lot going on here. Walking down the hallway, in addition to the shop were meeting rooms, some open, some closed. Slater peered in the glass panel of one of the doors at what looked like a twelve-step meeting, chairs in a circle, one person talking and the rest listening. They all looked like they lived here.

Homeless people were easy to talk to, if they were lucid, and lots of them had a vibe, a kind of essential honesty, like the woman in the shop, the way she'd looked him right in the eye. They'd already gone through all the bullshit, all the way to the very bottom, and didn't need to hang on, the way everyone else did, to the mass delusion that kept everything going—white Benzes, velvet fainting couches, fiddly little brass gadgets to shove up inside your kidney.

Farther along, on the opposite side, he glimpsed three school-age kids sitting at a table with a woman, and as he passed the open door, facing them was another person, with an idiosyncratic knot of gray hair at the back of his head—Dave. Slater stood near the doorway, out of view, listening.

"How do you know it's a verb?" one of the youngsters asked.

"The verb tells you the time," Dave said. "It says whether the sentence happened in the past, or now, or in the future."

Grammar, Slater thought. He was teaching them. Because it was here, with shelter kids, on Saturday, he had to be volunteering. That explained why he was comfortable parking that luxy Caddy on the street out front—people knew him here.

Heading back to the entrance, Slater acknowledged the security guard on his way out, and walked back to his office.

The Skid Row Residences, he found, sitting at his desk again, were a shelter more than long-term housing, and the website contained a long list of volunteer opportunities—food prep, teaching life skills to adults, and what he'd seen Dave doing, tutoring school kids with homework.

Checking the tracking app, Dave was moving again, and Slater watched the green circle flit along, south on the freeway but past Downey, past Dave's house, almost to the airport in Long Beach, where he stopped. It was a driving range, he saw, looking closer. No point in going down there, Slater decided. It didn't feel like it had anything to do with Derek Laird, and Slater did not need to watch this guy practice his golf swing.

———◆———

Later in the afternoon, after Dave's car had moved again, first to a drugstore, then home, he got a text from Max:

Where you at?

Slater texted back:

In the office.

Max's reply was concise:

Right on. Be there in 20.

Slater had to grin at his enthusiasm.
When Max arrived, Slater followed him into

his office and dropped into the chair in front of his desk.

"I hope your target was more interesting than mine—he wound up at a golf course."

"No sign of your boyfriend Laird," Max said, leaning back in his chair, "but I tailed Gwen to the Crenshaw District. A hair salon. She got an extremely expensive treatment, but to be honest, it looked exactly the same after."

"How expensive?"

"It's a high-end place where they only work on retainer—six hundred a month."

"You went in and asked?" Slater said, grinning at the idea of a big mooky white guy like Max walking into a hair salon for black women.

"Of course I did—after the target left. I talked to the stylist, and told her that my wife has very complicated black hair, and she's shopping for a salon, but she can't come in herself because she has social anxiety disorder."

"So smart," Slater said.

"Right?" Max said emphatically. "It's a legitimate condition, and it gave me a reason to ask about women's stuff without sounding like a masher."

"'My wife is an emotional wreck right now, and I need your help.' You're such an attentive husband."

Max chuckled. "After that, I watched her

head east again, but she went to the place on Mateo where she'd been all night."

"That's where she lives."

"I figured."

"Does six hundred dollars sound like a lot for an HR clerk to spend on her hair every month?"

Max looked thoughtful. "I guess it depends on what your priorities are. HR people are in charge of all the salaries, aren't they? Maybe she carved out a hair budget for herself."

"Maybe."

Max glanced at his phone. "Christ—it's later than I thought," he said, rising from his chair. "I'm meeting a potential new client."

"What does he want you to do?" Slater asked, getting up too. "Or is it a she?"

"He—and he wouldn't say."

"Probably a window-shade case."

"That's what I'm thinking. Anyway, I'll be around tomorrow," he said, and left.

Those were the sleaziest jobs they did, running surveillance on people to catch out cheating spouses. It usually wasn't necessary to actually peep around window shades, but the moniker was fittingly tawdry. Slater felt lucky right now to be on an insurance job instead, but Max didn't seem to think skulking around other people's romantic encounters was any less interesting than anything else they did, and that was fortunate—he did so many that it really was his bread and butter.

Sitting at his own desk, making some notes on his computer, clacking away at the keyboard, he heard a firm knock at the door. Slater froze. No one ever came here unannounced, especially on Saturday, when the building was quiet, most of the sewing factories off for the weekend. Locking his computer with a quick keystroke, he went to the front door and pulled it open. The man practically filled the door frame, dark and beefy and muscular, a royal-blue satin shirt showing his huge bulging pecs. His beard was carefully shaped and trimmed close, and he had way too much product in his slicked-back hair.

"What do you need, big guy?" Slater asked.

He puffed his chest out and asked gruffly, "Are you Ibáñez?"

"Might be," Slater said affably. "Who are you?"

"You need to stay away from Derek Laird." He spread his massive hands, gesturing widely. "Just let it go."

Slater put his hands on his hips and frowned. This guy was buff, and huge, but he wasn't from Slater's world. Glancing at his waist, there was no telltale bulge or pucker in his belt indicating he had a weapon tucked around back, so he was unarmed. He looked more like a bodybuilder than the heavy, just standing there like a dope, not in a stance ready to fight—unless he was a martial artist. But skilled martial artists were never musclebound, and they were usually really calm, confident in the knowledge that they could kick anyone's ass. This guy's chest was heaving, adrenaline surging. No, this was no martial artist; this was a civilian.

"Who told you to come here?" Slater demanded.

"You just do what you're told," he said firmly, and turned to leave.

"Hey," Slater said, following him into the hall.

The guy turned back, and Slater punched him in the face, spinning his head. He tried to twist away, but Slater hit him again, twice, in the ear and in the kidney, making him yelp and bend at the waist, protecting his stomach.

"Why do you make me hurt you?" Slater shouted, grabbing his right wrist and twisting it around behind him, up his back. The guy was strong, and he struggled to pull away, panting from the pummeling, but Slater had the advantage now, and increased the upward pressure, eliciting a cry of pain.

"Move it," Slater demanded, shoving him, stumbling, toward the fire exit, then slamming him into the wall. Even using all his force was ineffective at rattling such a massive and well-padded guy, but he didn't know how to use his bulk to fight back. Pulling open the stairwell door with his free hand, Slater grabbed his collar, whirled him around, and shoved him down the stairs.

He tumbled a few steps downward, arms flailing, and caught the rail, his chest slamming against it, and looked up at Slater, eyes wide, blood on his lip. There was more fear than anger in that face, Slater saw, which meant he wouldn't be back.

Slater jabbed a finger at him. "Don't tell me what to do."

The guy rose and hobbled down to the next landing, glancing up again but continuing downward. Slater listened to his footfalls, which were picking up speed, and once he was satisfied the guy was gone, went back to his office. Pulling his satchel over his shoulder, he locked up and went to the elevator.

The muscleman's visit was a good sign—it meant Laird wasn't involved with organized crime, or even basic habitual crooks, who would have sent a real heavy, someone like Max. The muscleman was a cartoonish exaggeration, a caricature of a guy like Max. He was probably just one of Laird's friends, but his appearance meant that Laird was getting worried.

———·———

Before he went to meet Rahim, Slater wanted to eat something heavy, as a buffer in case he drank at the party they were going to. Climbing into the Thunderbird, he drove to the Grand Central Market, finding a metered space out front, and went in to sit at the vegan ramen counter, where he slurped up the hot delicious noodles.

Rahim's street was more crowded with vehicles than it had been before, and he had to park a couple of blocks away. Climbing out, he reached into the backseat for his faux-leather jacket and pulled it on. He loved the way it looked on him, but he hated that it looked like leather, hated that contradiction.

On the street there were other people on foot, walking toward Rahim's house, where the front door was open, all the windows ablaze with light. It struck him then that the party was here—Rahim was the host.

It was already crowded when he went inside, with people occupying the furniture, standing around the kitchen, talking loudly. Most of them seemed to be around Rahim's age, and most of them were definitely straight, but at least there was lots of ethnic diversity. Slater looked for a familiar face among them, but there was no sign of Rahim, or the peroxide blond he'd been with yesterday, or anyone he'd seen at Ganesh.

The kitchen counter had become the self-serve bar, and he grabbed a Corona from the cooler on the floor below it. Standing in the living room, sipping his beer, he looked around, trying to figure out which guys might be available.

"You came," Rahim said, walking up behind him and slapping him on the shoulder. "I love your jacket." He was talking loud, and his eyes were bright, already a little buzzed. The guy-liner was a little heavier tonight too.

"You have a lot of friends," Slater said.

"It's from my work—sales is all about socializing."

A woman came up to them and grabbed Rahim's upper arm, demanding in a high voice, "You have to come and see Marshall."

Slater watched her drag him away, then wandered through the house and out into the backyard. There were a lot more people out here, standing on the grass and lounging on lawn furniture. A wood fire blazed in a little portable pit. Toward the back of the yard was an orange tree, or maybe a lemon; it was hard to tell from this distance in low light. It needed to be pruned, pronto, but it had good roots, based on the amount of fruit it was producing.

Scoping out the people, he managed to catch the eye of a chunky guy with a beard, standing near the fire pit.

"Hey," Slater said, raising his eyebrows, but the guy just nodded and turned back to the conversation he was in.

Looking around, it seemed like everyone

already knew each other, embedded in serious conversations.

Walking back toward the citrus tree, he saw Rahim talking to a group of three people, all of them listening intently, their eyes bright in the firelight. Rahim was facing them, so Slater couldn't hear what he was saying, but he could see they were hanging on his words. Watching them for a minute, watching Rahim's broad gestures, he had to smile. The guy was a born orator, a natural extrovert, and this was his element.

Slater walked back toward the house. Sitting on the railing that ran around the back deck was a pale woman with short black hair, puffing on a vape pen, her face glistening with sweat.

"Hey," Slater said, inadvertently catching her eye.

"Corona," she said, gesturing with her pen to the bottle in his hand. "You're saner than most of them."

"What are most of them drinking?"

"They were into the sloe gin. It's such vile stuff."

"I would have to agree. That doesn't smell like pot."

"Regular old tobacco," she said. "The scourge of society."

"Do you work with Rahim?"

"I'm a school friend. The name's Mary."

Slater introduced himself, and asked, "By school, you mean college?"

Mary shook her head. "Way back—high school. Are you Rahim's new boy toy?"

"Did he tell you that?" Slater demanded.

Her eyebrows shot up. "I'm just guessing. You don't look like a marketing guy. I'm not in that world either."

"What world are you in?"

"I'm a therapist."

"So is Rahim out with everyone?" Slater asked, glancing around the yard.

"I don't know about his corporate clients, but he's out with everyone who matters. Certainly with everyone here."

"Does he have a lot of boy toys?"

Mary grinned. "I don't want to be a gossip, especially if you're serious about him."

"The truth is always the best option, don't you think? I suspect you understand that, being a shrink."

"You're right," she said, bobbing her head in assent, then puffing on her vape pen.

"So what's Rahim really like?"

"Well, truth be told, that pretty face and gregarious demeanor are definitely strong assets."

"Looks and charm oil the gears?"

"And make him think he can do anything," she said, her eyes flicking toward the yard. "People melt for him, and believe whatever he says. He got into lots of trouble in high school."

Slater shrugged. "So did I."

"Yeah, but you look like you did. Rahim looks like the boy next door. And when he smiles, he looks like a little angel. You'd trust him with your grandmother's jewelry. It means he can get away with a lot more."

Slater considered that. It had the ring of truth, he decided, and aligned with what he'd seen himself.

A guy stepped out of the house and stood beside Mary, looping an arm around her back. He was dark, maybe South Asian like Rahim, and wore a loose white cotton shirt, his hair tied behind his head. Eyeing Slater, he murmured a greeting.

"This is Clay," Mary said.

"Are you a therapist too?" Slater asked him.

Clay frowned. "How did you know that?"

"I've known lots of shrinks over the years. You kind of have that vibe."

"What do you do, anyway?" Mary asked.

"Different things," Slater hedged, putting a hand on his hip and sipping his beer.

"Like a gig worker?" Clay asked, grinning at him. "What were you doing today before you came over here?"

"I punched a guy and threw him down the stairs."

His eyebrows shot up. "Is he dead?"

"Of course not," Slater said, frowning. "If he were, I wouldn't have told you that."

"You get paid to punch people?" Mary asked.

"Indirectly, yeah."

"I guess everything's monetized in some way," she said.

"Can you show me how to throw a punch?" Clay asked.

"Is that really something you need to know?" Slater said. "I do it because I have to."

"I've never done it," Clay said, "But I was reading this theory that the bones in our faces evolved to withstand punches."

Mary scoffed. "That implies that punching people is built into human nature."

"Interesting," Slater said.

Clay stepped away from the railing. "Come on—just for fun."

"All right," Slater said. "Show me how you make a fist."

"Boys," Mary muttered, and puffed on her vape pen.

Clay held out his right hand, tightly clenched, knuckles white from the pressure.

Crouching to set his bottle on the deck, Slater rose and manipulated Clay's hand. "Thumb over here," he said, moving it beside his fingers, "and don't squeeze your fist, just close it. Imagine you caught a ladybug, and you want to hold it safely in your hand, not squish it."

"OK," he said, nodding, and adjusted his grip.

"These knuckles make first impact," Slater said, tapping his index and middle fingers. "When you make contact, they should line up with your wrist, and your elbow, and your shoulder. Imagine they're connected in a straight line. That means the force of the blow won't dissipate sideways, and you won't crack your wrist."

"Complicated," he said, but shifted his elbow a little, frowning in concentration.

Slater adjusted his fist, twisting it with both his hands. "It starts out at forty-five degrees, and as your elbow straightens out, it rotates to horizontal." Gently pulling his arm out, he demonstrated the movement. "The force doesn't come from your arm muscles, but from your back and your pecs. Can you feel that?"

Clay extended his arm through the full range of the action, then again, practicing, feeling the movement. "I think so."

"Try it out—punch me."

Clay frowned. "Where?"

"Either shoulder," Slater said. "It's hard to do much damage there."

"You're not allowed to punch him back," Mary said pointedly.

Standing in front of him, Clay furrowed his

brow in concentration, then threw his fist, connecting with Slater's left shoulder.

"Not bad," Slater said, "but don't lift your shoulder—it rotates forward, not up. And use more force."

"I don't want to hurt you," he said.

Slater frowned with mock concern. "I've got good health insurance."

Clay wriggled his fingers, balling them up, then struck again, hard enough to twist Slater's arm backward.

"Excellent," Slater said, grinning and rubbing his shoulder. "Now you can work over your patients."

"Dude," someone called from the lawn, "What did you say to him?"

It was meant to be humorous, Slater knew, but he wasn't here to be a spectacle. "It was nice to meet you both."

"Thanks for the lesson," Clay said.

Mary waved good-bye with her pen. "I hope things work out with Rahim."

Slater picked up his Corona and went inside, draining the bottle and leaving it on the kitchen counter. The living room was even more crowded now, and he maneuvered through the sea of bodies and out the front door.

Behind him, someone shouted, "Hold up."

It was Rahim, jogging after him to the

sidewalk. When he caught up, he said, "You just got here. I saw you talking to Mary—did she say something to scare you off?"

"It's nothing to do with her."

"So what's going on?"

Slater shrugged. "Your friends are cliquey, and boring."

Rahim's eyes narrowed. "Are my friends boring, or are you just entitled and intolerant?"

Slater slapped his face, hard, and then back on the other side, a firm kovac.

Taking a step back, Rahim suddenly looked more sober, holding his cheek. "Do you get off on doing that?" he demanded. "Does it give you wood?"

"Go on back to your party," Slater said, jutting his chin toward the house.

"I'd rather go with you." He moved closer, grabbing the lapels of Slater's jacket and pulling him closer.

"What about your guests?" Slater said, leaning into him for a moment, feeling the warmth of his body.

"They won't even notice I'm gone."

"I'm thinking more about them jacking your stuff. You have nice things."

"They're my friends—they're not going to steal from me. Most people are basically decent."

"Where I come from," Slater said, "most

people are basically fucking crazy. If you're not there, they'll trash your place and rob you blind."

Rahim watched him for a moment with a sad smile. "When you're a hammer, everything looks like a nail." He let go of Slater's jacket. "I'll call you this week."

Slater turned and walked toward his car.

Too mainstream, he told himself as he drove home. Way too mainstream to be boyfriend material. He had to shut it down. The guy was so handsome, though, and the sex was hot.

He was too tired for a hookup, he decided, climbing the stairs from the garage, but something almost as good was waiting. Pulling off his jacket, he hung it on the back of the door, then pulled out the bourbon, admiring its rich luminosity. Taking a long pull directly from the bottle scorched his throat, and he coughed and gasped, wiping his mouth, and then poured a tumbler.

With the lights out, he stretched back in the recliner and turned on the radio. Saturday night house music. His mind was already unspooling—he could feel it—and in a minute he'd be completely into the groove, synchronized with the rhythm.

He gazed at the dark room, the strip of sky above the building across the street. Saturday night, and Slater was completely alone. But that was stupid sentimentality. With a few swipes at his phone he could have a warm body over here in minutes if he wanted to. But even then, he'd still be alone—just him, alone inside his head.

NINE

His muscles ached but he wasn't nauseous, thankfully, when he woke up, naked and in his own bed. Grabbing his phone, he checked on idiot Conrad. He was at home, probably sleeping in, the lazy schmuck. Why did he even bother to check on him when the guy was so irritating?

Rahim was home too, he saw, or at least his phone was. No surprise there—he was probably wiped out from his party. Dave was at his house in Downey, and Gwen's car was in the Arts District, but not at her place. The location-estimate green circle on the map encompassed a parking lot and a gym. Seeing her working out was definitely not worth a trip over there.

Rising, he started a mug of water in the

microwave, then drank from the kitchen tap. After he swirled the brown powder into the mug, he took the ersatz coffee to his recliner and sipped at it, resting with his eyes closed.

On his chest his phone vibrated, and he picked it up to see that Dave's car was moving. As he watched, it moved to a street not far from Ganesh's building, where it stopped. Slater zoomed in to see where he was. The only structure within the little green circle was an Irish pub.

It was a good opportunity to talk to Dave, he realized, in a public place and away from Gwen. But Slater hated Irish pubs. True dive bars were for loners, and even though Irish pubs were usually dives, they were also thoroughly sociable, which seemed like a messed-up combination. They were usually full of Aussies too, and Aussies loved to fight. Maybe it would be calmer at noon on Sunday—the real drunks would still be asleep.

Pulling on his jeans and a clean shirt, Slater headed down the stairs and drove to Downey, mostly on the freeway. On a timeworn commercial street, the pub sat on a corner, fronting an apartment building.

Slater fleetingly wondered if Dave might be in there rather than at the bar, but when he pulled into the lot, Dave's distinctive Eldorado was parked near the pub's entrance. Between the apartments and the bar was a hedge of bougainvillea with a riot of fuchsia bracts in it, growing up through a chain-link fence, and Slater admired it as he climbed out of the Thunderbird. If he lived next to an Irish pub, he'd plant something like that too, an impenetrable wall of thorns to keep the drunken brawlers at bay.

Stepping inside, he spotted Dave right away, sitting on his own at the bar. Coffee cup in hand, he looked up as Slater walked in.

Dave's eyes narrowed. "Ibáñez? What are you doing here?"

"I wanted to talk to you away from your staff," Slater said, walking over to him.

"So you followed me?"

"I was driving by, and I saw your car. There's only one of those around. That's quite the paint job."

Dave chuckled. "I never have trouble finding it in a parking lot." Dave watched him for a moment, then said, "Sit down."

Slater took the adjacent stool and waved at the bartender, ordering a pint of ale and dropping a twenty on the counter. Despite Doris's pointed reservations about him drinking during the daytime, it didn't break his booze rules: he'd just have the one, and he was with people.

"Someone said you drive an old car too," Dave said.

"It's a '78 Thunderbird. And I prefer the term *classic*."

"Fair enough. Women love a guy in a classic car."

"Yeah, well, I only date guys," Slater said, frowning.

The bartender set down Slater's beer and took the twenty.

"A man's man," Dave said, nodding. "I didn't pick up on that. Bully for you. I know you guys have more fun than we do."

"I could show you fun," Slater said, eyeing him. "Settle up your bar tab—I'm parked right outside."

Dave laughed, the lines deepening around his eyes. "I know I'm supposed to say that's inappropriate, or something like that, but honestly, I'm flattered. You hit a certain age and nobody flirts anymore."

"With you? I find that hard to believe."

"In any case," he said, holding up his palm, "thanks for massaging my ego, but it's not going to happen."

The bartender put Slater's change on the bar in front of him, then poured steaming black java into Dave's cup from a bulbous old-school carafe.

"Are you drinking coffee in a pub?" Slater asked.

"I come for the food," he said, nodding at the

empty plate sitting on the bar, with a smear of ketchup and the remnants of something deep-fried on it. "Caffeine is as strong as it gets for me. I quit drinking twenty years ago."

"Court ordered, or by choice?"

Dave chuckled, cradling his cup. "Things were rough, but I never had to stand before a judge."

"Why did you quit?"

"Anyone in recovery will give you the same answer: using was screwing up my life."

"When do you know that it's screwing you up, though?" Slater said. "Having a hangover once in a while isn't so bad."

"It was more than hangovers for me. I was a full-blown addict. I lost my job as a nurse because they don't like you sampling the meds. When that happened, my wife decided she'd had enough, and packed me off to a rehab in the Miracle Mile."

"Those Lubavitch guys?"

Dave frowned. "How do you know about that?"

"I've run across them before. My mother would love to get me into a place like that."

"So you're Jewish." Dave studied him for a moment, sipping his coffee. "I could see that. It's not every day I meet a blue-collar Jew."

"I don't need you to label me," Slater said, glaring at him.

"Relax, son," he said, glancing down at Slater's hand, which he'd absently balled into a fist. "Why does your mother want you to go to rehab?"

"She thinks I drink too much," he said, looking back to the bar and picking up his beer glass.

"Well, you won't ever regret quitting, I can tell you that." He pulled a card from his pants pocket. "That has my cell number on it. Call me if you ever want help with sobering up."

Suppressing his anger, Slater gritted his teeth and stared at the card for a second, not reading it but willing himself not to react, then stuffed it into his pants.

"That's not why I'm here," he said finally. "I want to know why you changed your tune on Derek Laird."

"Isn't it odd that he won't meet you?" Dave said. "He claims he's emotionally debilitated, but you said he's not even home. That means he's out somewhere, doing something. That doesn't sound like someone who's debilitated to me." He sighed, swirling the contents of his cup. "At some point people have to face the consequences of their actions."

"I'll drink to that," Slater said, and lifted his beer glass. "So you don't care one way or the other if we pay Laird or cut him off."

"I don't wish him any further misfortune. He did good work for me, but I paid him well for it.

As far as I'm concerned, we're even, him and me. From now on, he has to take care of himself, don't you think?"

"What about Gwen—what kind of employee is she?"

"What's your interest in her?" Dave said, sipping at the contents of his cup.

"I need to know how she's involved with Laird. I know they're connected outside the office."

His brow furrowed. "I don't know anything about that. Gwen's thoroughly competent at her job."

"Not a drag on morale?" Slater asked, watching him.

"HR is always the bad guy, as far as employees are concerned. Beyond that, she's not universally disliked, as far as I know."

"You're not chummy after work?"

"That would be no," he said firmly.

"You pay her well?"

"Not as well as Laird," he said, eyeing Slater. "She earns a competitive salary."

Slater killed his beer, then pocketed some of his change, leaving a few dollars for the bartender, and rose from the stool.

"That's it?" Dave said, frowning. "You just came by to grill me?"

"And to have a beer," Slater said, before turning toward the door.

"Son?" Dave called after him. "Lay off the applejack."

Slater turned back. "I'm not your son," he said, and walked out.

Just because you're dry and don't know how to have fun anymore doesn't give you a license to be passing out lifestyle advice. Thinking about Dave's words, Slater had to grin. Nobody today would be brewing up illicit snow-country apple-jack, especially not around here. It wasn't even in his bloodline—his mother's ancestors had been urbanites, not frostbitten Northeastern orchard dwellers, and Slater's father's people were from El Salvador; they would have been making *aguardiente* in the tropical sun.

Glancing around the parking lot to make sure he was alone, Slater crouched beside the plum-colored Eldorado and reached up into the wheel well, locating his tracker and prying it off. Climbing into the Thunderbird, he tossed the device on the floor in the back, then navigated to the freeway in the light Sunday traffic.

His phone buzzed, and he glanced at it to find that Gwen was on the move. She was on surface streets downtown, he saw, checking from time to time as he drove, and then the circle went gray, the way it had with Rahim—she'd gone into a subterranean parking lot. Based on where she'd disappeared, it had to be the one under Pershing

Square. From there she could be going anywhere, but Slater was close, not more than a couple of minutes away, on the 110 between his neighborhood and downtown. He deftly changed lanes and roared onto the Sixth Street ramp.

His luck held as he raced up to the square moments later: Gwen was standing on the corner, waiting to cross Sixth, holding hands with another woman, shorter and dark. They wore matching track suits, deep purple, the color of a heliotrope in bloom in a well-watered garden, in dressy velour, the kind you'd get dry-cleaned and never wear to do anything that might actually raise a sweat. Matching outfits—this had to be her girlfriend. Slater leaned back in his seat as he cruised by, but Gwen didn't notice him among the stream of other vehicles. Of course she wouldn't; there was no reason she'd be looking for him, or looking into cars.

There was a surface lot in the next block, he knew, but he didn't even have to go that far. Seeing an SUV pull out just past the square, he quickly swerved into the space. Not sure if he had to feed the meter on Sunday, he didn't pause even to check the signs, climbing out of the Thunderbird and hustling down Hill Street, scanning for his targets. Had he lost them? But soon he caught sight of the matching purple outfits, on the other side of the street, walking into a jewelry store.

Slater trotted across between the cars and slowed his pace, strolling past the windows of the shop. Gwen and her companion were wandering along the display cases inside, the whole interior brilliantly flooded with blue-white light. It must make the jewelry pop, that kind of lighting, because all these shops used it.

The women stopped in front of a clerk who was standing behind the counter, an older guy with a pot belly and a rug that didn't match the color of the hair protruding below it. The guy spoke to them earnestly, gesturing with his hands.

Feeling eyes on him, Slater looked to the shop's entrance, where the security guard was assessing him. Nodding in acknowledgment, Slater pretended to be absorbed in the bling on display in the window. He wanted to hear what they were saying, but it was risky—if Gwen looked up and saw him, his whole surveillance operation was burned. But the two of them were thoroughly absorbed in whatever the clerk was saying. The guy stepped away, but Gwen and her partner stayed put at the counter until he returned a moment later with a tray of something sparkly.

Walking toward the door, Slater looked the security guard in the eye and said, "How are you?" It was usually the best way to allay suspicion, and it worked now—the guard just nodded at him and let him pass. Slater studied the contents of another row of display cases, keeping his back to Gwen, listening.

"Forty thousand?" Gwen's girlfriend said. "That seems like a lot."

"Diamond's aren't pedestrian," the clerk said, "and they're not like a car, or a handbag—stuff that you wear out and throw away. This piece will last a lifetime. You can leave it to your children. Until then, you'll look like a goddess."

A woman approached Slater from the other side of the display case. "See anything interesting?"

"Not yet," he said quietly. "I'll call you if I need your help."

"Just give me a wave," she said, and stepped away.

Gwen was talking to the clerk. "Can you do any better on the price?"

"Let me check," he said, and in the periphery of his view, Slater saw him walk toward the back of the shop.

"If you like it, let's get it," Gwen said.

"You're too good to me, baby."

Slater turned his head to see them from the corner of his eye. Based on what Rahim had said, that they'd been together for years, she was likely the same woman that Gwen had choked out and sent to the hospital. He wondered if expensive jewelry made up for that kind of behavior.

"I can come down to thirty-eight five," the clerk said, returning.

"Let's do it," Gwen said. "It looks so lovely on you."

Slater had heard enough, and walked to the doorway, out onto the street, heading toward the square. It was a huge parking lot, but he should be able to find Gwen's car before she got back to it.

Trotting down the stairs, he quickly strode the aisles, scanning for the white Benz. It took a while, but he found it, finally, along the outside wall, pulling out his phone to double-check the plate number with the photo he'd taken of it at Ganesh. Glancing around to make sure he wasn't being observed, he squatted beside the rear tire, reaching into the wheel well and retrieving his tracker, then standing up and slipping it into his back pocket.

He'd only made it a few steps from the car when Gwen and her girlfriend appeared, walking toward him. Before he could turn and disappear between the vehicles, she'd spotted him, a suspicious frown clouding her face. Slater sighed and kept walking toward them.

"Fancy meeting you here," Gwen said, arching her heavily made-up brows.

Slater looked pointedly at the paper bag dangling from the other woman's hand. "Out shopping today?" he asked Gwen. "It's not really the neighborhood for it, unless you're buying jewelry."

"I'm Tina," the other woman said, furrowing her brow, her tone demanding acknowledgment. "Gwen's wife."

Slater introduced himself, adding, "Gwen and I have some business dealings."

Gwen's eyes narrowed, flicking toward her car.

"What brings you down here on a Sunday?" she asked.

"My office is nearby," he said casually, and to Tina, "What's in the bag?"

Tina frowned. "What are you, the shopping police?"

"Have you made any decisions about Derek's coverage?" Gwen asked.

"I need to meet with him first. You certainly haven't helped make that happen."

"We should go," Tina said, walking past Slater.

Gwen followed her, the lighthearted air she'd had in the jewelry store gone.

Slater watched them walk toward the Benz, then headed to the stairs and up into the square. When he was a few steps beyond the top of the stairwell, Gwen called from behind, "Ibáñez."

"Are you following me?" she demanded.

"Looks more like you're following me," he said, hands on his hips. "Why would you be worried about that? Have you got something to hide?"

"I don't know what you think is going on," she said, raising her voice, "but you need to respect boundaries. If you want to see me, I'm at my office nine to six, Monday to Friday."

In the periphery Slater noticed that they'd caught the attention of a diminutive woman, standing a few yards away, and she started to wander closer. Glancing at her, he saw that she wore a uniform, but not that of a cop; she was a private security guard.

Tina appeared at the top of the stairs to the garage, still carrying the jewelry bag.

"Gwen," she shouted. "Let's just go."

Gwen held up a finger to her, not looking, still glaring at Slater. Walking toward the stairs, a man in a blazer glanced sidelong at them, his expression a little worried, and then stepped around Tina, disappearing into the stairwell.

Slater turned to the security guard and shouted "Security," which brought her hustling over. She was easily a head shorter than him.

"I'm afraid for my personal safety," Slater said to her as she approached.

The guard stood with her hands on the front of her belt and looked at Gwen, then dubiously at Slater. "You are?"

"Please don't let them stalk me while I leave the area," Slater said. Pointing to Tina, he added, "Her henchman is over there, in the matching outfit." Turning away, he walked back toward the Jewelry District.

"Asshole," Gwen shouted after him.

"Ma'am?" the guard said, her tone authoritative. "What seems to be the problem?"

Slater grinned to himself. Gwen wasn't very savvy, shouting abuse at him in front of a security guard. Those people made very credible witnesses if things went sideways later on.

Not far away was a short alley that had a couple of delis in it, including one that made a wicked black olive and hummus sandwich, and Slater ordered one, sitting outside to eat at a little table, surrounded by the tall backs of the neighborhood's towering buildings and the long shadows of the end of the day.

Gwen was a big spender, dropping forty grand on diamonds, all nonchalant, as if she were buying socks. Plus she had that hair stylist on retainer. It seemed like excessive spending for someone on an HR director's salary. Was Laird subsidizing her? Not as a romantic partner, given that Gwen was full-time with Tina, but maybe something else was going on. Maybe she had something on Laird, and was bleeding him dry, keeping him away from Slater in case Laird spilled the truth.

She'd figured out that Slater had been following her too. That was his fault; he'd been sloppy. He should have abandoned his search for her car when it took so long. The realization had unnerved her, naturally enough. But maybe instilling a little fear in her would shake things up, maybe even shake out Derek Laird.

Finishing his sandwich, he pulled out his phone and checked the camera in Laird's apartment. There had been no activity, as far as he could tell, with the mishmash of Cyrillic and broken English in the app, and when he turned on the live view, he saw only a grainy low-light image of the faucet over the kitchen sink. Laird hadn't been in the apartment for almost a week. The guy had to be living somewhere else. The only solid lead he had was from the tax return—the property in Big Bear.

Finding Laird's number, he dialed and got the generic voice-mail greeting. "It's Slater Ibáñez," he told the machine. "Where are you, Derek? I know you haven't been at your apartment. I still need to talk to you. Things are going to go south for you fast if you don't deal with this. And what's with the muscle man? Did you honestly think he could intimidate me? This isn't amateur hour. I hate to drop the *f* word, but this is starting to look like fraud."

Walking back to his car, he was glad to find it without a parking citation, and double-checked the signs to confirm Sundays really were free.

He drove the few blocks to his office, finding the building quiet.

Once he was upstairs, on his computer, he looked up the land location from Laird's tax return. A satellite map showed a blurry square roof at the coordinates he'd listed, but it was all alone in the woods, with no outbuildings, no cars parked nearby. There wasn't even a road, just a narrow double track that ended at the cabin. A single-track trail continued beyond it.

Zooming out, he traced the wider track to the end of a paved road, a residential street lined with roomy spread-out lots. These were getaway resort houses, typical of Big Bear, but why was Laird's off on its own on a dirt road? It might not even be drivable in the Thunderbird. The street view of the paved road revealed a metal gate across the access to the track, clearly marked NO VEHICLE ACCESS. Not a gate, he realized, as there wasn't a corresponding fence: it was just a vehicle barrier between two trees. Pedestrians could easily get around it. Looking at the map again, it was maybe two miles' walk from the end of the road to Laird's cabin.

His phone rang, and when he glanced at it, he saw that it was a number in an area code he didn't recognize, and the only info provided by the caller ID was "Alabama." It was probably spam, but he picked up anyway.

"I got your message," a man's voice said.

"Derek?" Slater said. "You're starting to piss me off. We need to talk."

"We're talking now."

"You know what I mean."

"I went out of town, so I can't really sit down with you."

"I'm supposed to believe you're in Alabama?" Slater scoffed. "I'm thinking this number will turn out to be as fake as your cell number. I know what spoofing entails, Derek. It's so straight-forward that even a simple-minded accountant could figure out how to do it."

Laird was quiet for a moment, then said, "I'd understand if your company needs to void the coverage and stop paying my disability."

"That's not how this works," Slater said. "Where are you really? At Gwen's place? I know you're tangled up with her somehow, but she seems to have a full-time wife, so I doubt she's screwing you."

"What are you talking about? I haven't seen Gwen since I left Ganesh."

"That's a lie," Slater said flatly. "Is she black-mailing you? If you're in this with her, you need to watch your back. She choked out her wife with a bunch of little kids watching."

"How do you know about that?" Laird demanded.

"Are you up at Big Bear? That seems more plausible than Alabama."

"What?" Laird said, his voice rising. "I don't know what you're talking about."

"Yeah, you do," Slater said. He could hear it in his voice, even in low-resolution audio.

"I'm going to hang up now," Laird said. "Do what you need to do with my payments, but you need to stop harassing me. Leave Gwen out of it too."

The line went dead, and Slater swung his feet up on his desk, gazing at the faded painting of the artichokes on his office wall. Anyone who would encourage him to stop sending them money was definitely hiding something. Laird was being protective of Gwen too, and he'd even used the same awkward phrase she'd used, "void the coverage." They were definitely colluding, he decided. Mentioning Big Bear had also touched a nerve. Slater needed to go to that cabin. Not in the dark, though; he'd go tomorrow.

Right now he needed a hookup—it had been days. Even though he lived just a couple of miles away from his office, the app presented a different crowd than in his neighborhood, he saw, scrolling through the faces. On average the guys were whiter and more affluent. There were lots of pricey condos and upscale hotels downtown, so even though the homeless population living on the streets outnumbered the homed by four to one, they weren't the ones showing up in the hookup app.

A guy without a torso picture, just a head shot, caught his eye. With the thin lips, dirty blond hair swept back in a money haircut, suit jacket over an open shirt, he looked like Rahim's bleached blond from the bistro. Slater texted him:

> In your neighborhood. I want to make you scream.
> No drugs.

Slater went back to flipping through more faces, and a reply came:

> You look hot. I'm staying at the Baltimore. Come on over.

He'd already been in that damn hotel once this week, and it was back where he'd just been, surveilling Gwen and Tina, but at least it was on the way home.

> Be there in 10.

Slater rode the elevator down to the street and across to his car. Not willing to overpay to valet park at the Baltimore, he parked under Pershing Square, like Gwen had, and drove past the space where he'd found her white Benz. Coming back here felt like repetitive behavior, self-destructive and aimless, he thought, climbing up the stairs into the square.

Walking through the grand lobby to the elevators, then up to the fourth floor, Slater found the guy's room and rapped on the door with a knuckle.

When he pulled it open, he looked exactly the same as in his app photo.

"Wow—you really came," he said, his eyes wide.

"Are you going to ask me in?" Slater said.

The guy stepped aside for him to enter, then closed the door behind him. The room was bigger than the one he'd been in when he'd been posing as Miguel; it must be a suite.

"You're wearing the same jacket as in your photo," Slater said, turning back to him. "Did you just take it?"

"About three minutes before you messaged me. I've never done this before. I'm kind of shocked that it worked so quickly."

"What's your name, rookie?"

"Griffin," he said.

That didn't sound made up, Slater thought, looking him over.

"Look at you," Griffin said, shoving his hands into his pants pockets.

Slater decided to hold off pawing him. "You seem nervous."

"I guess a little. It's different when it's real, rather than all theoretical on my phone."

Slater nodded, looking around the space. On the desk were a set of keys and a wallet, along with a simple gold ring. He really was new at this, leaving all that out in plain view. Also on the table was a wooden sculpture of a duck, and Slater picked it up, turning it over in his hands.

"Do you always travel with your duck?"

Griffin chuckled. "I got that today. Right downstairs. I was inducted into a professional guild. A duck for in*duct*ion, get it?"

"Funny," Slater said. "What profession?"

"I'm an architect."

"Why aren't you down there celebrating with your peers?"

"I wanted to do my own celebrating." He went to the minibar and stooped, pulling it open. "Do you want a drink? Or is that included in your no-drugs policy?"

"Do you see applejack in there?"

Griffin studied the selection for a second. "Nothing quite so exotic, I'm afraid."

"I don't need anything, then," Slater said. "I'm not worried if you do." Setting the duck back on the table, he resisted the urge to pick up the wallet and flip through it.

Griffin twisted open a mini bottle of vodka and drank from it.

"So where are you from, Griffin?"

"Uh ... San Francisco?"

Slater nodded. "Bullshit."

"What, I don't look California enough?"

"It's your delivery. Listen, it doesn't matter to me. It's fine if you want to be anonymous. I see you left your ring here—so are we cheating on a wife, or a husband?"

Griffin frowned. "It's not like that."

"I get the feeling you don't do it a lot, so let's make it count. What do you want to do?"

Griffin quickly finished the vodka. "I don't know."

Slater put his hands on his hips. "Yeah, you do. You just don't want to say it because you think it's too insane. Everybody's sex thing is insane, Griffin. But I'm the guy you can explain it to."

"Well ..." he hesitated. "What do you want to do?"

"I want to taste the vodka in your mouth, and then take your clothes off, and run my hands through your hair. Eventually I want to fuck you. Unless you need to be in charge—in that case, you can fuck me."

Griffin stepped closer. "I like the sound of all of that."

Bolder now with his Dutch courage, Griffin kissed him, tentative at first, and then getting into it. The sweetness of the vodka was still on his tongue, and Slater ran a hand into his hair, feeling his cock tightening in his jeans.

"Do you have condoms?" he asked.

"Oh, no," Griffin said, dismayed. "I never thought of that."

"These places always have them. Just call the concierge."

"Really?" he asked, biting his lip.

"They're not going to tell anyone, or print it on your bill. Do you want me to do it?"

Griffin nodded, and Slater picked up the phone beside the bed.

"You must do this a lot," Griffin said, after Slater had replaced the receiver.

"Not a lot," Slater said, eyeing the woody in Griffin's suit pants, "but I know what I'm doing."

Unbuttoning his shirt, he pushed Griffin onto the bed, locking their mouths together. He had Griffin half undressed when there was a sharp knock at the door. Griffin started as if he'd had an electric shock.

"Give them a tip," Slater said, watching him climb off the bed.

"Really? How much?"

"I don't know—five bucks."

Grabbing his cash from the desk, he peeked around the door, returning with a brown paper bag with the top stapled shut. Grinning, he stood at the end of the bed and dropped his underpants.

Slater watched him, hands behind his head. "You're pretty proud of yourself, huh."

"Can I take off your jeans?"

"Hop to it, son," Slater said.

Griffin climbed up next to him and unbuckled his belt, gently sliding his pants down, then took Slater into his mouth. Slater closed his eyes, enjoying the intensity, but eventually grabbed his head, pulling him off.

"If you want me to fuck you, you have to stop."

Griffin moved up and kissed him, his skin sweaty, his mouth hot and yielding. On his side, Slater ran his hands over his back and his legs, gradually working his fingers into him, then pushing his cock inside. Leaning into it, Griffin moaned, his eyes screwed shut. Slater breathed in the scent of his hair, pounding him until he came.

When he pulled out, Slater took hold of Griffin's cock, one arm around his neck, kissing him hard, and stroked him until he came too.

They lay there for a while, Slater facing the room with Griffin behind him, one arm around his chest.

"It's still early," Griffin said. "Do you want to go get dinner somewhere?"

"I ate before I came over. I should go soon."

"OK." He was quiet for a while, then said, "So why did you say 'no drugs'?"

"There are lots of meth-heads on the hookup apps," Slater said. "People are more fun when they're sober, and they're less likely to rob you. Be wary of that if you do this again."

"I'm not planning on making it a habit."

"You can't just switch off your libido," Slater said, sitting up and shifting to the side of the bed. "I'll leave you my card. Call me if you're in town again."

Lying in bed, watching him get dressed, Griffin looked forlorn. Slater went back to kiss him good-bye, massaging his arm and his shoulder for a minute, pressing their foreheads together, trying to make up for whatever he'd missed, whatever it was that Griffin had wanted but clearly wasn't getting.

"I wish I could make you feel better," Slater said quietly.

"You could stay."

"I can't," he said, and as he left, dropped his card on the desk, on top of the gold band.

Darkness was falling as he drove home, and he flicked on his headlights. It was barely dark when he got into his apartment, but still, it fit his rules: he was in for the night, so he could start drinking. Filling a tumbler from the bourbon bottle, he dropped in an ice cube and stretched out in the recliner. He needed to get up early, he reminded himself, so he couldn't get too tight.

He set an alarm on his phone, then started a *Sasquatch Search* podcast, sipping the heady golden liquid and getting lost in it, following the quest deep into the woods.

TEN

Waking to his alarm, it was a relief that his head felt clear, and he got dressed, in a work shirt he wore to do Doris's gardening—he was going into the woods today, after all. In case it was out of cell range, he downloaded a map for the cabin and the trail from the paved road. He didn't have a lot of experience in the wilderness. No way did he want to get lost.

Backing out of his garage, he pulled around to a gas station in his neighborhood to fuel up for the drive, and from a woman selling tamales on the corner bought a potato-and-onion one to eat later in the car. It would only take two and a half hours or so, his phone told him, and he followed its instructions, getting on the freeway, heading east. Feeling no sense of urgency in the bright morning sun, he drove calmly, acclimating to the flow of the traffic, not pushing.

The transition from urban to countryside was quick and dramatic, and he was on a winding mountain road almost as soon as he left the freeway. It was a beautiful drive through the forest, and the highway was quiet. Once he was up top, in Big Bear, the route skirted the lakeshore for a while, in view of the dark-blue expanse, and soon his phone told him to turn off the highway. A couple of additional turns led him into a sparsely populated mountain neighborhood, where the driveways grew farther apart as he ascended. It seemed drier and rockier than he remembered, the pines shrubby and sparse, but then he'd only ever been up here in winter, and it had been years ago.

Eventually there were no more driveways, no houses visible, and the road dead-ended at the familiar barrier across the head of the dirt track. No other vehicles were here, he realized, parking his car at the side of the road. Did that mean Laird wasn't at the cabin? The barrier had a padlock on it, and it was hinged to swing open. If the track was private, maybe Laird unlocked it and took his wheels in with him.

Climbing out, he stretched his back and stood for a minute, inhaling the scent of the pines on the thin dry air. The sun seemed brighter than in the city, and the only sound was birdsong and the buzz of insects. Glancing back at his car, he started off, walking around the barrier onto the trail. It was clear of vegetation, but the surface was rocky and rutted. Even if he could open that gate, no way could he drive the low-slung Thunderbird on it. Soon he was out of view of the barrier, trudging along, alone in the forest.

The track was ascending, gradually, and Slater realized he was breathing hard. He wasn't used to hiking, but the elevation must be part of it too. Most of the sasquatch sightings he'd heard about on the podcast were much farther north, in denser, more humid forests, but there had been isolated sightings up here, in Crestline, even closer to the city. The witness said the creature made a kind of whooping sound, and that it marked the forest subtly with broken branches, maybe even using branches and twigs as a form of language. That wasn't useful information; Slater had no experience in this world, and wouldn't be able to tell an intentionally positioned twig from one that nature had put there at random.

Bigfoot rarely caused anyone any grief, so there was nothing to be afraid of, even if he could overhear it, or even see one. Stopping for a minute to listen, not really expecting to hear the giant cryptid, he realized that this is what those questers were talking about, how they felt out here, the singular tranquility, so different from the city. The sigh of the breeze coursing over countless pine needles was infinitely calmer than the subsonic rumble of traffic ever could be. It was easy to understand why people found it relaxing—there were no people out here, so there was no danger.

It took almost an hour to get to the cabin, and as he walked into the clearing, he saw instantly that the overhead photo had been misleading. There was indeed a roof, but no walls, just posts at the corners holding it eight or ten feet off the ground. Under it was bare earth. It was an open-air shelter, not a cabin, and it wasn't inhabited by Derek Laird or anyone else.

Uneven ground nearby implied that there might once have been other structures, and a few yards behind the shelter was a fire pit with the charred remains of logs, broken glass, and a few bottle caps. Next to the trail was a wellhead with an old-fashioned hand pump that wasn't really old—the mechanism was free of rust, the pipes painted bright blue. Slater wandered toward it, surveying the site.

This was a place to pitch a tent and camp, not a country getaway cabin. But it was the right spot; he knew it was. The trail that went higher into the forest was narrower than the one he'd hiked in on, just as he'd seen on the map. Even so, he pulled out his phone and checked his location.

There was no cell signal, but the GPS data was unequivocal; this was the land that Laird was deducting property taxes for.

Not finding Laird hiding out here made it feel like a wasted trip. Why would he be paying taxes on a useless freaking campground? It was four acres of nothing, difficult to get to even if he had a four-wheel drive and could unlock the barrier at the bottom of the track.

Slater walked a circuit of the shelter again, scanning carefully in case he'd missed something. When he came back to the trail he caught sight of a hiker heading toward him from farther up. It was the first person he'd seen since he'd left his car. Watching the guy approach, he saw he was wearing a tan shirt with a shoulder patch and a little brass badge—a forest ranger. Tall and fit, the guy was in his fifties, maybe, and wore wraparound sunglasses, and of course he was Anglo. Why were there so many freaking white people once you left LA?

The ranger seemed affable enough, calling a greeting to Slater, but then he stopped, sizing him up.

"You don't look like most of the people who come up here," he said.

"Because I'm not blond and blue-eyed?" Slater demanded. "It sounds like you're profiling me."

"Because you're not dressed for hiking, and

you don't even have a day pack. What are you doing up here?"

"How could that possibly be any of your damn business?"

The guy put his hands on his hips. "I'm the equivalent of law enforcement in this forest. It's my job to know what people are up to."

"You're also not armed."

"I do have a radio, though, and I'm pretty sure I can guess where you parked. If you want to talk to someone who's armed, I can arrange for them to meet you."

"Settle down," Slater said, waving a palm. "There's no need to get steamed. I work for an insurance company, and I'm investigating the guy who owns this place."

"That would be your Uncle Sam."

Slater frowned. "What are you talking about?"

"This is national forest land. It went out of private ownership in the 1970s."

"Are you sure about that?"

"Dude—look at my uniform. I know my territory. Whatever parcel you're looking for, you got the location wrong. Does it look like anyone's been living here?"

Slater looked at the empty structure. "Damn it."

"Backpackers camp here, and through-hikers use the shelter in the summer."

"So I've been played."

"What's the guy's name? I live down the hill, maybe I know the family."

"Derek Laird."

"Never heard of him. Is he in trouble?"

"Maybe," Slater said. "I can't seem to track him down, and he's clearly not here."

The ranger nodded. "Will you be able to find your way back to town?"

"I should be able to handle it," Slater said flatly. "This isn't exactly the Donner Pass in February. You might help me with the water pump, though. I don't have a bottle. Can you crank the handle so I can get a drink?"

"Sure," he said, stepping over to the pump, breaking into a smile.

"What's so funny?" Slater demanded.

"You've never seen one of these before?"

"No, but I know what it is."

"You can pump it yourself and still get a drink. There's a delay in the mechanism—it flows for a while after you stop working the handle. But I'll help you anyway."

He heaved on the pump handle, and Slater cupped his hands under the spout, startled at how cold the water was, once it finally started gushing out, and drank deeply, eventually stepping back, wiping his mouth, and shaking the water off his hands.

"That's enough, Stretch," Slater said, annoyed that the guy was still grinning, that he'd found Slater's inexperience so entertaining. "Do you ever get lonely out here?"

"With all this majesty?" He waved an arm at the trees. "Never." Then his head snapped back, looking at Slater. "Wait—are you propositioning me?"

"That's where I was headed, yeah."

He frowned, his earlier amusement evaporating. "I don't swing that way, son. You'd best go on back to your vehicle."

"Thanks for your help," Slater said, and headed back down the trail.

The hike back was easier, as it was mostly downhill, and before he'd expected to see it, the barrier and the paved road came into view. He climbed into his car, hot inside even though it had been parked in the shade, and blasted the air-conditioning. The drive back to the metropolis felt easier too, coasting downhill on the narrow winding road.

Slater knew he hadn't gotten the location wrong, knew it was the right place. That meant the tax return had been bogus. Laird had picked a random point on a map, or maybe picked the roof of the derelict structure, too remote for anyone to bother going to check out. It was pretty nervy, claiming public land as a deduction, if that's what he was doing, trying to scam the tax people.

Once he was out of the mountains, it took an hour of intent driving on the freeway to get downtown. Slater never drove like a knucklehead, but he drove hard now, changing lanes whenever he could get a speed advantage. On the 10, somewhere around Alhambra, he saw the towers of the Financial District looming in the distance, languid hulking shapes in the haze. *Civilization*, he thought. Home. He took a deep breath, feeling his entire body relax.

Parking at his office, he climbed out and stretched, then headed across the street, checking his phone to see the notification he'd ignored on the freeway. It was the camera in Laird's apartment—someone had been inside. Max wasn't in the office, he saw as he came in, and Slater sat at his own desk, turning his phone sideways to watch the recording.

In the video, the room lights flicked on, momentarily washing out the image, but the camera quickly adjusted, revealing the sink. Gwen stepped into the frame, dressed for work in a dark suit and full makeup, almost raccoon-like in the shadowy lighting. She had the white clock in hand, the one with the camera that Max had disabled, and she set it on the countertop. As she stepped closer to the camera, her belt filled the video frame, and when she stepped back again, she was holding the box of breakfast cereal Slater had seen in the cupboard.

Gwen opened it and shook a few handfuls of cereal into the sink, then turned, presumably putting the box back where she'd found it. Next she went to the fridge and returned with the carton of milk. She poured some into the sink and then ran the tap, flipping on the disposal for a second. After she put away the milk, she picked up the dishes that were stacked on the towel beside the sink, replacing them with different clean dishes from the cupboard—two mugs, spoons, and a glass with a bowl leaning on it.

Grabbing the camera clock, she stepped out of view, and the lights went off. The video ran for a few more seconds and then ended. Slater stared at the frozen final frame, a still image of the empty kitchen.

She'd taken the clock camera. It was Gwen's, not Laird's. Dumping food down the disposal, then walking right out again. His heart pounded with the creeping realization—she wanted to make it look like someone was still living there, and she wanted to see who came in to check. Even the tax return must have been her, must have been for his benefit. She'd sent him on a freaking wild goose chase. He really had been played.

Gazing at the artichokes on the wall, he went through what he knew, thought about what to do next. Before he could act, he needed more information, a few more data points to confirm what he thought was happening, and that meant a visit to Della. Her office was only a few blocks away, and he was sick of sitting behind the wheel of the Thunderbird. Walking over there would give him a chance to clear his head.

It was a quick walk through the Fashion District and the fringes of Skid Row to the towers of the Financial District. Strolling into the lobby of the office building that was home to Cudahy Mutual, Slater rode the elevator to the thirty-fourth floor.

"Hey, Crystal," he said, catching her eye as he approached the reception desk. "Do you want to tell Della I'm here?"

She frowned at him but picked up the phone, after a moment saying, "Mr. Ibáñez to see you."

Slater waited in front of her desk, hands on his hips, watching her.

She hung up and said, "Go on back."

"Thank you," he said, feigning sincerity, and walked toward Della's office.

Her door was open, and when he rapped on it with a knuckle, Della looked up and beamed at him. Today she was wearing a dark-green satin blouse with a string of pearls over it.

"I'm glad you're treating Crystal like a human being," she said.

Slater dropped into one of the chairs in front of her desk. "Your whole system is an impediment to getting anything done. If you don't want to see people, put a deadbolt on your door."

"You've never worked in an office, have you," she said, her eyes narrowing.

"Lucky for you," Slater said. "I'm out there busting your fraudsters instead."

She leaned back in her chair. "Is that what you've found in the Laird case?"

"I think so. It might be worse than just fraud."

Della frowned. "Like what?"

"I'm not sure yet. Did you see the news last week? I did some digging into Lynn Cheung, the doctor who signed all of Laird's claim paperwork. She's definitely crooked."

"I heard about the woman she dumped at the Baltimore. I wondered if you were somehow mixed up in that. They said the concierge found her."

Slater nodded. "Miguel. He's a friend of mine."

"I don't suppose I want to know the details," Della said, raising her eyebrows.

"It doesn't matter how I was involved. Her assistant performed the lipo on that woman, using Cheung's name."

"Seriously?" She shook her head in disbelief. "Even so, it sounds like Cheung is the one going down for it."

"What I don't get is why the medical board wouldn't have kicked her out by now, what with almost killing a patient through neglect, plus the opioids investigation."

"It's run by doctors. They're not going to turn on one of their own unless it's something that gets a lot of attention. They'll censure Cheung when she gets convicted of something."

Slater sat forward. "Listen, can you tell me where the insurance payments to Laird are going? The mailing address."

"It should be easy enough to find out. I'll have to make some calls. Can you wait?"

"Of course," he said, and pulled out his phone as she made the call.

Conrad was at work, the dumbass, Slater saw when he checked, and so was Rahim, in Downey.

Jotting notes on her blotter, Della made a second call, reciting Laird's name again. Finally she hung up.

"Laird doesn't get a check," she said. "His payments are directly deposited to a bank account."

"What kind of bank account?"

"I don't have the number, but his name is on it." She glanced at her notes. "It's at the Downey Orange Growers Bank."

"I know where that is," Slater said, then rose, stuffing his phone into his pants.

"Is it a useful detail?"

"I think so," he said. "Thanks—I'll be in touch."

"Always a pleasure," she called after him.

As Slater passed the receptionist's desk, Crystal looked up, her expression clouding at the sight of him. He kissed his palm and tossed it toward her, loudly saying, "Mwah."

Walking back to the office, he stopped at a sports bar to eat. It wasn't the kind of place he'd normally go, but everything they served was vegan, and it was on the way. Even though it was broad daylight outside, the bar was noisy and full of drinkers, spilling onto the patio. A century ago this whole neighborhood had been banks and corporate offices, and it still had that vibe, beaux arts and art deco, even though these classic buildings now housed residential lofts and places like this. Slater sat at the bar to eat, ordering a couple of greasy pub appetizers, but didn't drink anything—he needed a clear head for what was going to happen this evening.

Once he was in his office again, he pulled out his phone and dialed Rahim.

"I felt bad about my party the other night," Rahim said when he picked up.

"Because I left?" Slater said. "You don't need to worry about me. I can take care of myself."

"Mary said you taught her boyfriend how to punch people."

"So there you have it—proof that I was

enjoying myself. Listen, I want to see you. Are you around tonight?"

"I can be, if it's for fun. I'm leaving work in the next few minutes."

"I'll swing by your place?"

"Unless you want to eat somewhere."

"I ate already," Slater said, and ended the call.

Squatting in front of the safe behind his desk, he pulled open its heavy door and found the handcuffs. Max had a couple of pairs of the cop version stored here, but Slater's were more restrictive, the two sides hinged together rather than linked by a chain. He made sure he had the right key on his keyring, then slid them into his hip pocket.

ELEVEN

n the evening traffic the drive to Downey took twice as long as it would have late at night, the 10 a sea of brake lights, every lane crawling in waves of stop-and-go congestion. When he finally pulled up in front of Rahim's house, he climbed out and opened the trunk, grabbing a roll of duct tape.

"It's open," Rahim called when he knocked.

Slater stealthily set the roll of tape on the table beside the door as he stepped in, then locked the deadbolt. Still dressed for work, Rahim walked toward him. Scanning the room, Slater saw that his wallet and his keys were on the kitchen counter.

Rahim slid his arms around Slater's waist and kissed him, and Slater kissed back, feeling his dick swelling in his jeans. Before he got too into it, he pulled away, reaching for the handcuffs in his back pocket and holding them up, dangling from his finger.

Rahim grinned. "You're pretty kinky."

"Do you have a sturdy chair?"

"Like the ones at the dining table?"

"That'll work," Slater said, and walked over to the table, pulling out one of the chairs and setting it in the middle of the living room floor.

Rahim embraced him again, more turned on now, pressing his woody into Slater as they kissed. Eventually Slater grabbed the sides of his head, pulling back.

"That looks like an expensive shirt," he said.

"It is."

Slater gestured with his chin. "Take it off."

Rahim unbuttoned it, watching him. "I assume I'm the one getting cuffed?"

Slater took the shirt and threw it on the dining table. "Sit down," he said firmly.

Rahim did, and Slater squatted behind the chair, pulling his wrists around and squeezing the cuffs on, lacing them behind one of the chair's vertical bars. It was solidly built—Rahim wouldn't be able to stand up without taking the whole thing with him.

Standing in front of him again, Slater admired his torso. Forcing his arms behind his back highlighted the definition in his pecs.

"You're so hot," Slater said, and went back to the front door for the duct tape.

Rahim's eyes narrowed. "What's that for?"

Peeling off a length of it with a loud squawk, Slater dropped to one knee and looped it around his left ankle, binding it tightly to the leg of the chair.

"You're putting tape on my pants?" Rahim asked, concern creeping into his tone.

"Trust me—you do not want this stuff on your skin," Slater said, and taped his other ankle.

It was sturdy enough, he decided, checking his work, and then rose and went to the kitchen counter. Flipping open Rahim's wallet, he pulled out the cards one by one, examining them and then dropping them on the counter.

"What are you doing?" Rahim demanded, craning to see.

"And here it is," Slater said, holding up a card and waggling it at him. "Downey Orange Growers Bank. A credit card with Derek Laird's name on it, but your signature on the back."

"There's nothing wrong with that," Rahim said, alarm in his tone. "We have a financial relationship."

Slater dropped the card on the counter and stepped back in front of Rahim, winding up and delivering a powerful right hook to his mouth. Rahim's head snapped to the side.

"Where's the body?" Slater demanded.

"What the fuck, man?" Rahim shouted. He worked his jaw, scowling at him, fear in his eyes.

"I asked you a question," Slater said, and struck him from the other side, again snapping his head.

"What the fuck are you talking about?" he whined. "What body?"

Slater struck him again, open-handed this time, but hard. "You and Gwen killed Derek Laird and set up the insurance scam. What did you do with his body?"

"I never killed anybody," he said, wriggling in the chair and straining against the cuffs and the duct tape, but it was useless—he wasn't going anywhere.

Slater cocked his head, watching him. The fear in his eyes seemed authentic. But he could just be a good liar. His friend Mary had said as much at the party. Slater slapped him again, full force. A trickle of blood dropped out of Rahim's nose.

"Stop it, you fucking psycho," Rahim screamed, twisting in the chair. "Let me go."

"You know, that's hurtful," Slater said, putting his hands on his hips. "In middle school my shrink always said not to use words that were labels. People are more complex than that. I'm actually showing some serious restraint here, not psychotic behavior. I haven't broken anything. Not yet. But

I'm going to start, brother, if you don't sing."

"I didn't kill anybody," he shouted.

"Why is Derek Laird's credit card in your wallet?"

Rahim eyed him, silent, breathing hard. Slater balled up a fist and moved to punch him again.

"Wait," he shouted. "Just stop. It's Gwen—it's all her doing, all her idea. She's the one who planned it."

"That doesn't answer my question."

"I helped her, OK? There it is."

Slater sighed. "It doesn't answer the question about Laird. What did you do with his body?"

Rahim leaned forward, straining against the cuffs. A lone drop of blood struck the floor in front of him. He closed his eyes for a moment, breathing hard, before he spoke.

"Laird never existed. Gwen invented him to suck money out of the company."

Slater scoffed. "Bullshit. You rolled him into the trunk of your Beamer and planted him out in the Mojave. I know Gwen wouldn't put a body in the trunk of her car—it might stain the carpet."

"I don't know how else I can say it," Rahim said, raising his voice. "Laird's not real. He never was."

Slater examined his knuckles, studied the blood on his hand, then rubbed it into his other palm.

"Wait," Rahim shouted, snapping upright. "Just wait. What evidence have you seen that Derek Laird ever existed? You never met him."

"I talked to him," Slater insisted.

"Did you really? Think about it."

Slater watched him, considering that. He'd talked to Laird on the phone. Really, it could have been anyone. Plus the number was spoofed. Was there something to this? Slater stepped back, looking around the room, lost in thought. Rahim's soulless catalog furniture, creating a false impression, a lifestyle he didn't live. The bookshelf full of books chosen for the color of their spines, books that no one would ever read. Laird's out-of-state driver's license could have been faked, and even Dave had never met Laird face-to-face.

Slater turned back to Rahim. "If that's true, who did all the clever accounting work?"

"Sophisticated software. The clerks at Ganesh were told they were entering data for Laird to work with, but it was for the software to work with. It's AI-driven, so it communicated with the staff intuitively, the way a person would, using real language. It cost only a fraction of what Ganesh paid Laird."

"You administered the software?" Slater asked.

"It didn't need administering, but Gwen handled it. That's how she got the idea: 'Imagine an accountant letting this software do everything,' she said, 'and then sitting around all day not working.' She's in HR, so it was easy to set up a fake employee."

"Dr. Cheung," Slater said. "She met Laird, and diagnosed him, and signed off on his disability."

He shook his head. "She signed off because she was paid off. She never met him either."

"If he doesn't exist, why did he need an apartment?"

Rahim took a deep breath, calmer now that the threat of further blows was fading. "Things got more complicated once we committed to it. There was no turning back—we had to make him seem real."

"Laird would have had to sign things, and show up for audits. One of the women in accounting had lunch with him."

Rahim shook his head. "No, she didn't. Laird was all Gwen. She signed his name, even faked his fingerprint when she notarized things. That was easy; she was the notary."

"Why did you help her?"

Rahim looked away. "You know why."

"I'm not psychic," Slater said sharply.

"Money," he said quickly, leaning back in the chair, sweat glistening on his pecs. "Free money. It seemed foolproof. Dave was clueless." He closed his eyes for a moment, breathing heavily. "I wanted to end it, and Gwen agreed, but then

she had to take one last dip—the disability insurance. We almost panicked when Cudahy Mutual
started digging. But then you came along. We
thought you were too stupid to figure it out."

Slater stepped closer and slapped him, open
hand, just hard enough to make his head spin.

"You love this," Rahim said, his lip curling
into a sneer. "You're in your natural element."

"I'm good at it," Slater said. "That doesn't
mean I'm enjoying it."

"I can see your stiffy in your jeans. You're
totally turned on."

"That's about you, sitting there with your
shirt off. Not about the interview."

"Interview." Rahim scoffed. "Why don't you
uncuff me, then, if you like the view, and we can
mess around?"

"No," Slater said absently, looking around the
room again. He needed to parse all this.

"You're holding me against my will," Rahim
said, raising his voice.

"Nope. I'd explain it was just a sex game gone
a little too far. There's evidence of our ongoing
relationship—photos from a few days ago of my
dick in your mouth."

Rahim frowned. "You never took any photos."

"Are you sure about that? Shut up for a minute. I need to think."

"Even if you don't have photos like that, I

won't call the cops. Just unlock me."

"If you don't shut up, I swear I'll tape your mouth shut."

Rahim glared at him, but kept silent, his face hot.

Slater walked toward the front window, looking through the sheers at dusk descending on the quiet street. Finally he turned back.

"I need to hear Gwen explain it."

Rahim scoffed. "Good luck with that."

"You're going to call her, and tell her that I want a cut of the action to keep quiet about it."

"Most of it is already spent. There's nothing to give you."

"There's the disability payments."

"She'll never go for that," Rahim said.

"But she'll come over to talk about it, right?"

Rahim glared at him. "Why should I help you? You just beat the shit out of me."

"If I'd beaten the shit out of you, you'd be in a coma and on a ventilator right now. You're not bleeding anymore, and you won't even have bruises—I made sure of that. I couldn't bring myself to mar that pretty face." Slater watched him for a moment. "You need to look at things differently, brother. I'm actually helping you right now. If you don't get her to talk, you'll go down for this alone, and she'll skate."

"So you're going to tell the cops?"

"That's not my plan, but I will if I have to. My concern is recovering what Cudahy Mutual has paid out to a dead man."

"A fictional man," Rahim said intently.

"Are you willing to get her to come over here?"

Rahim pressed his mouth into a tight line, but he nodded.

Slater told him what to say, then went to the kitchen counter to get his phone, unlocking it with the code he'd used before. Dialing Gwen, he held it up to Rahim's head.

"How did you get into my phone?" Rahim demanded, eyeing him sidelong, but then Gwen answered. "You need to get over here," he said. "The cowboy figured out what we're doing, and he wants a cut."

Rahim winced at her screaming, leaning away from the phone.

"I never said anything," he protested. "He's smarter than he looks, OK? I'm meeting him at my place tonight." He listened for a moment, then nodded at Slater to hang up.

"So?" Slater demanded.

"It'll take her a while to get here. She's in Ventura."

"Why would she be up there? I know she was at work today."

He huffed in frustration. "Why does anyone go there, Slater? It's Ventura."

"The cowboy—is that what you call me?"

"It's because you always wear denim."

Slater nodded. "If I unhook you, what are you going to do?"

"Wash the blood off my face, for starters. What do you want me to do?"

"What we started before our interview. But this time, you're going to fuck me. Maybe work out some of that aggression."

His eyebrows shot up. "OK. We've got at least an hour and a half."

Sliding Rahim's phone into his pants, Slater went to the kitchen counter and pocketed his keys as well. He pulled a knife from the wooden block beside the stove, then put it back and found a smaller one. None of them looked like they'd ever been used.

Crouching in front of Rahim, he eyed him and said, "You're not going to take off?"

"It doesn't seem like there's much point. I just saw you take my car keys."

Slater cut the duct tape at his left leg, peeling it away from the wood. "Are you afraid of Gwen?"

"A little, maybe. She can be tough when she wants to be."

"Do you know if she has a weapon?" he asked, moving to the other ankle and slicing through the tape.

"I never heard her say anything about guns."

Stooping behind the chair, Slater unlocked the cuffs, folding them and sliding them into his hip pocket.

Rahim sighed in relief, wriggling and stretching his fingers, rubbing his wrists.

"You're a real prick sometimes, you know that?" he said, glaring at Slater.

Slater watched him as he worked his hands.

"I know," he said quietly, and offered Rahim his hand.

Pulling him up, he took Rahim's wrist, massaging it gently where the metal had left red imprints, then kissed it. Rahim leaned into him, letting him support his weight. They stood that way for a few breaths, until Slater pushed him up again, herding him to the bedroom, where he pulled off his own clothes and draped them on a chair. Rahim stood watching, arms folded, until Slater sat on the edge of the bed and pulled him over, undoing his belt.

"I'm sure you ruined these pants," Rahim said, hands on Slater's shoulders. "Duct tape won't ever come off."

"I saved your shirt, though."

Pulling his trousers down, Slater took him into his mouth, working his cock until he was rock hard, then pulling back, resting on his elbows.

"So what are you going to do?" Slater asked.

"I'm going to fuck you," he said quietly.

"Pardon me?" Slater demanded, cupping a hand to his ear.

"I'm going to fuck you," he said, louder, and climbed on top of him, reaching into his crotch and kissing him.

He rose briefly to get a condom and roll it on, then grabbed Slater's thighs, pushing him up and penetrating him. Rahim gasped with the intensity of it, building up his rhythm.

"Fuck," he mumbled.

"What did you say?" Slater demanded.

"Fuck," he said, louder.

"Fuck who?" Slater insisted.

"Fuck you, you psycho."

"What did you call me?"

"You're a psycho," Rahim shouted, pounding him. "Psycho. You fucking psycho."

He came, roaring, and collapsed on Slater, who grabbed his own cock. It didn't take him long to come.

Rahim wrapped his arms around him, holding him tightly, one knee between Slater's legs. As he caught his breath, his nose buried in Rahim's hair, Slater felt the intense warmth of his body. This guy was so beautiful, he could hardly stand it.

TWELVE

Eventually Rahim pulled away and climbed out of bed, heading toward the bathroom. Slater watched warily in case he went for his phone or his keys in Slater's pants, but he didn't, and soon he heard the shower go on. Slater found a towel and cleaned up, then got dressed, and went to the living room, sitting in one of the sterile stylish lounge chairs, waiting for Gwen.

Rahim came out of the bedroom and clicked on the room lights. He was wearing chinos and a polo shirt, his hair wet, the guy-liner washed away.

"Why are you sitting in the dark?" he asked, dropping into the other chair.

"I don't know," Slater said. "I guess it felt right."

"I wish you'd give me my phone back."

"Not yet."

Rahim didn't reply, and they sat in silence for a while.

"You look miserable," Slater said finally.

"I was just wondering if that's the last time I'll have sex outside prison."

"Is that where you think you're headed?"

"Of course it is." He frowned. "When this comes out, my life is over, Slater."

"You made a mistake, but it's not the end of the world. Right now you have to hustle to minimize the impact."

"What are you talking about?" he demanded, but then the doorbell rang.

Slater rose and pulled out his mini voice recorder, and started it, then set it on top of the bookshelf at the side of the room. He waved Rahim to the door, then watched as he went to open it.

Gwen stepped in, again wearing a dressy track suit, brown and tan, gold necklaces dangling down the front and a handbag slung over one shoulder. When she spotted Slater, her eyes hardened. "What did you tell him?" she said, not looking at Rahim.

"I didn't tell him anything," Rahim said, closing the door and walking back toward Slater.

"You were sleeping with him," she said, raising her voice. "You were just supposed to distract him, not blow up the whole operation."

"I think you may have underestimated my skills," Slater said calmly.

"However it is that you found out," she said, "there's no way you're coming in on this."

Rahim spread his arms. "Gwen, it's over—"

"Shut up," she snapped.

"Relax," Slater demanded, and put his hands on his hips. "I just want to talk."

Reaching into her handbag, Gwen pulled out a pistol, fumbling to get a grip on it, and then leveled it at him. Her hand drooped with the weight, and paradoxically, its appearance made her appear less confident.

"What are you doing?" Rahim said, alarmed.

"Is that a forty-five?" Slater said. "Good god, woman, are you planning to take on a SWAT team? Don't point that thing at me."

Now that she'd produced it, she didn't seem sure about what to do next. In her plan, this must have been the ultimate move. But she had no idea how to use the weapon, Slater saw, with her finger on the trigger, and the manual safety engaged. Slater wasn't so close as to be absolutely sure, but it looked like a P90, or a close relative, and the lever was in the safe position—if he remembered correctly.

"What is it with you people and guns?" Slater said.

Gwen frowned, engaged once again. "What

do you mean, 'you people'?"

"Lowlifes and crooks. You're always packing heat."

"I'm not a crook," she said hotly. "You watch your tongue." She waggled the weapon. "This thing puts me in charge."

Stepping slowly toward her, Slater knew he was taking a risk. He wasn't convinced she hadn't done away with Derek Laird, and if she was even a little familiar with what she was holding, she could instantly flip off the safety and ventilate him.

"You don't want to murder anyone, Gwen," he said calmly. "Mistakes have been made, but I don't think that's who you are."

"Stay back," she snapped.

Slater took another step, holding out his palm, holding her gaze, and then another. From this distance he could see a tremor in the ugly metal sheen of the weapon, the tumult of her nerves transmitted into it. She was no killer. Another step, and he took hold of the barrel, gently pulling it down, pulling it from her. Gwen just glared at him and let him take it.

Popping out the magazine, Slater saw that it was fully loaded.

"Where did you get this thing?" Slater demanded. "You could have killed someone." He met her eye. "Your wife is lucky you weren't packing this when you choked her out that time."

Her mouth hardened into a taut line, and Slater shoved the weapon into his belt in the small of his back. Moving closer to her, he slapped her hard, left then right, a rapid kovac.

Gwen stepped back and held her cheek, shouting at him. "What are you doing? I gave you the piece."

"That's for pulling a gun on me," he said. "If you'd tried to pull the trigger, I'd have flattened you."

"Maybe I should have," she said, glaring at him. "Shot you, I mean."

"You can't shoot anybody with the manual safety engaged," he said flatly, and gestured to the sofa. "Let's sit down and chill out a little, shall we?"

Gwen frowned, not moving. "You don't get to tell me what to do."

"Would you rather talk to the cops, and maybe explain where you got this heater?" Slater demanded. "Move it, sister."

She watched him for a moment but then looked away and moved to the sofa. Slater gestured for Rahim to sit too, then pulled over a barstool from the kitchen counter, setting it beside one of the lounge chairs, and sat facing them across the coffee table.

"So what's the price for your discretion, cowboy?" Gwen asked, jutting her chin at him.

Slater eyed her. Things were changing fast—a

moment ago she wasn't going to let him in on it at all; now it was negotiable. And she still thought she was in charge.

"First, you need to convince me you didn't kill Derek Laird," he said.

Rahim exhaled audibly. "This is such a fiasco."

"Would you shut up?" Gwen shouted at him. "Just shut up." She turned to Slater, recovering her calm veneer, and shot him a satisfied smile. "Derek Laird never existed."

"Are you sure about that?" Slater said, folding his arms. "He exists in the national identity database—I checked. So any cop who looks for him will find the record of a real person. As far as the IRS is concerned, he's an ordinary taxpayer. He's got an apartment, credit cards, IDs. Dave thinks he's real, and Jasmine in accounting too. Claudia swears she had lunch with him once."

"It's all made up," Rahim said. "I told you that."

"If that's what really happened," Slater said, "it's an impressive accomplishment. But if I told the police that he's missing, and that you two have been siphoning away his funds, why wouldn't they start a murder investigation?"

Concern furrowed Gwen's brow. "I invented all of it. Those records are all electronic. You just need one point of entry, and the rest falls into place."

Slater gestured widely. "Prove it. Otherwise

you're going to have cops pulling up these floorboards, swabbing your trunk for blood, and interrogating your wife and her kids."

"Slater," Rahim insisted, "I told you Laird wasn't real."

Slater looked at him. "It's almost like you're surprised that I won't take you at your word." And more sharply, "Why would I, when you've been lying to my face since the moment we met?" He turned to Gwen. "I talked to Laird on the phone, but the only photo I've seen of him was on a Pennsyltucky driver's license."

"Kansas," she said, frowning. "My sister works in vital records for the state government there."

"And she can just print up a bogus driver's license?"

Gwen nodded. "Sure. The trick is in creating a birth registration entry in the system, and then it's easy to create a driver's license record. Kansas is the Wild West with oil and gas right now. All those new arrivals are overburdening the state infrastructure, and it's a deep-red state—they cut way back on taxes, regulation, public services. There's hardly anybody working for government agencies anymore, and certainly nobody working to notice her sleight of hand."

"Who's the guy in the photo on the license?"

Gwen grinned. "It's from a website. This AI generates head shots of people, and the website asks, 'How real is this face, on a scale of 1 to 10?' It's interactive crowdsourcing, like a science experiment. There are images of hundreds of people who never existed. Maybe thousands."

"Show me," Slater said.

"Where's your computer?" Gwen asked Rahim, rising.

"Sit down," Slater snapped, and waited as she dropped back onto the sofa, scowling at him. "Rahim gets the laptop."

Rahim stood and went to the bedroom. While they waited, Gwen crossed her arms, avoiding Slater's gaze.

When Rahim sat down again, she gave him the name of the website, and Rahim found it, handing the laptop to Slater. He spent a minute clicking around on it. It was just as she'd described—an AI attempting to render photorealistic faces. Some were a little odd, but they all looked like real photos, real people. Finally he folded the laptop closed, setting it on the coffee table.

"What's your sister's cut?" Slater asked.

"None of your business."

"What about Lynn Cheung—if Laird is fictional, who did she diagnose?"

"No one," she said, throwing up her hands. "She's totally corrupt. For ten grand she'd sign anything."

"That came back to bite us, though," Rahim said.

"How so?" Slater asked.

"She wanted a second payment," he said. "She would have kept at it too, bleeding us dry. It was a nightmare."

"It wasn't a nightmare," Gwen said, looking at him askance, "because I shut her down."

"How did you manage that?" Slater said.

"I reminded her that if she blew up my racket, she'd go down too. No way could she claim that she'd actually met Derek Laird. Signing all those insurance documents meant she was complicit from the get-go."

Slater stared at her for a moment. "Who sent the muscle man to my office?"

Gwen sighed. "His name is Tony. He's a friend of mine from the gym. Why did you have to hit him? He needed stitches in his lip."

"He shouldn't have threatened me," Slater said simply. "He's lucky I didn't break his arm."

"You're a damn bully," she said.

Slater ignored her, watching them absently while he thought it through. It was a clever con, if that's what it was, creating the guy's presence with fake IDs, a fake apartment. He'd seen Gwen staging the place, dumping breakfast down the disposal. Laird's income discrepancy, the bone-headed nonhuman accounting mistakes that

Jasmine had described, and Laird always working from home. Nothing he'd seen contradicted their story, he decided. And it explained why a guy making seven figures had such a run-down little apartment.

That was the thing about the truth—it stood out because it was so rarely presented, elegant in its inherent lack of distortion, patiently knitting the world together. Derek Laird was a mirage, he saw that now.

"Where's your phone?" he asked Gwen.

"I am not giving it to you," she said, raising her eyebrows.

"Just show it to me."

She frowned but pulled it out of her bag, setting it on the coffee table. Slater pulled out his own phone and dialed Laird's number. A moment later Gwen's phone buzzed, and the screen came to life, displaying Slater's name.

"Why was your voice so much deeper when I talked to Laird?" he asked.

She shrugged. "Software. It's called pitch modulation."

Slater nodded. "OK. So Derek Laird's not real."

Rahim sighed, throwing up his hands. "Thank you."

"Tell me about Laird's property in Big Bear," Slater said, ignoring him.

"How did you know about that, anyway?" Gwen said. "Were you in his apartment? The memory card was missing from the camera. I couldn't figure that out."

"Was it meant for me, that tax return?" Slater said. "A way to get me out of town?"

She frowned. "It was for the IRS. Did you actually go up there?"

"It's not really even a building, and it's part of a national forest. Did you really think you'd get away with deducting it?"

"If you use the right software, you never get audited." She grinned, unable to conceal it, proud of how clever she'd been. "Besides, taking those risks would never come back on me. They'd be looking to audit Derek."

Slater put his hands on his hips and looked from one of them to the other. "Have you ever walked into a stand of bamboo? You two are like that."

Rahim's brow furrowed. "What are you talking about?"

"Nothing else grows where it grows—just bamboo stalks and bare earth. It's eerie, in a way. That's like you, Rahim. With your friends, you're a rock star, outshining all of them."

"OK," he said evenly.

"Bamboo looks like a bunch of individual trees," Slater continued, "but every stalk is a shoot of the same plant, with shared roots, identical DNA. You two and Derek—three people, but not really. Just one basic grift with the same messed-up deviant DNA."

"It sounds like you're trying to insult me," Gwen said.

"Just an observation," Slater said. "What's most interesting about bamboo is that it only flowers once every seven years. The flowers are huge, and white, and dramatic, and they drop off when they're at their fullest, before they start to wither. No sensible farmer would be anywhere near a stand of bamboo when it's in flower. Beautiful perfect blossoms dropping like that is symbolic of an untimely end."

"Like us," Rahim said quietly, eyeing him. "Like Derek."

"Bamboo," Gwen said flatly. "That's so interesting. But you still haven't told me what your buy-in is."

"To your scam?" Slater said. "I'm not interested."

"So you're going to the cops?" she demanded.

"I don't care about the cops. They can do their own work."

"So what's the problem?"

"This is such a good scheme, Slater," Rahim added. "So lucrative. Just slow down, and think about it for a minute."

"No dice. I'm going to tell Cudahy Mutual that Laird isn't real."

"Why would you do that?" Gwen insisted. "You don't strike me as the high-minded moral type. Just leave it alone, and I'll make it worth your while. Don't mess up my business—don't do that to me."

"It's not personal, Gwen. I don't care whether you live or die. But what about Dave? It seems to me that he's a decent guy, and you're robbing him blind."

Gwen rose, snatching up her phone. "Screw you, cowboy," she snarled, and headed toward the door.

"Wait," Rahim called after her. "Gwen—we need to talk this through."

She ignored him, pulling open the front door, and was gone.

"You just let her leave?" Rahim said. "You have the gun."

"I got what I needed from her," Slater said, rising from the stool and retrieving his voice recorder from the bookshelf. He sat at the other end of the sofa, facing Rahim, shifting position when the weapon cut into his back.

"What do you think she's going to do?" Rahim said.

"If she's smart, she'll go abroad before the roof caves in, and never come back. She knows it's over, but I just told her she has some breathing room. That gives you a chance to act."

"Breathing room?" Rahim said. "Because you're not going to the cops?"

"Exactly."

"How does that help me? The way I see it, I'm totally screwed."

Slater shrugged. "You might get off with no jail time if you play your cards right."

"How?"

"Go to the cops yourself and tell them what you've done. The insurance company will call them in once I make my report anyway, but it might take a few days. Tell them it was all Gwen's idea, and she dragged you into it."

"That's not exactly how it went down," Rahim said.

"It doesn't matter. Tell them you were afraid of her, and she coerced you to do it. She has a police record of using violence on people, so it's believable. You're not making it any worse for her—this is going to be bad for Gwen, no matter what—you're just making it easier on yourself."

Rahim nodded, looking away.

"Then when you talk to the DA's office, tell them you'll testify to everything to put her away, on the condition that they drop or reduce your charges."

"Does that really work?"

"It'll be much easier on you if you make a deal first," Slater said. "And whatever you do, don't tell Gwen any of it, not even a whisper. Don't talk to her again until you've done it."

Rahim sighed. "You think that's my best option?"

"Can you afford to abandon your life here and live in a nonextradition country?"

"I couldn't do that. It would be the same as being in prison."

Slater leaned toward him. "We all have extremely limited options all the time. People don't usually see that, but it's true. Make the best choice you can."

Rahim met his gaze. "Can you go to the cops with me? You seem to know how it works."

"No way." Slater shook his head. "That would be a massive conflict of interest. Go in with a defense lawyer. They know way more about cutting deals than I do."

"That actually makes sense."

"You and me, buddy—we can't hang out anymore either."

Rahim met his gaze. "Maybe when all this is over?"

"I'm not the guy for you. I'd make you unhappy."

"You can't know that."

"I know myself." Slater rubbed his eyes. "You

need to be with a guy like the blond from the bistro."

"Mike?"

"That's the one. He'd be good for you."

Rahim sighed, looking away. "Thanks for all the free advice." He dropped his head back on the sofa. "Why did I let this happen to me?"

"You said it yourself," Slater said, rising. "Greed. I'd move quickly with the cops—Cudahy Mutual is going to hear about this tomorrow, and so will Dave."

Slater pulled Rahim's keys and his phone from his pockets and set them on the coffee table, then went to the front door. Looking back inside as he let himself out, Rahim was still on the sofa, watching him leave.

He'd wait until tomorrow, he decided, walking to his car, before he wrote up his report for Della. Then he'd call Dave, and meet him at that Irish pub, buy him a coffee, and break the news, maybe play him the recording he'd just made of Gwen if he didn't believe it at first. Right now he had to get rid of this damn firearm, jabbing him in the back. Why were lowlifes so enamored of those?

Opening the Thunderbird's trunk, he looked around, then pulled out the weapon and put it under the floor mat. He stretched his back, glad to be rid of it, before he climbed in behind the wheel. The only loose end now was his attraction to Rahim, and he knew how to shake that. There were lots of guys around, and even better, there was always bourbon.

Also from Dagmar Miura

That First Heady Burn

The first book in the Slater Ibáñez series sees Slater running surveillance on an injured tech worker and tangling with blackmailers, party girls, late-night hookups with a gamut of guys, and a lot of bourbon.

slater.dagmarmiura.com

The Mason Braithwaite Paranormal Mystery Series

No one is ever quite sure whether psychic investigator Mason gets results with actual psychic power or his more mundane flatfooting, but the disheveled redhead manages to resolve some intractable mysteries.

mason.dagmarmiura.com

The Margarita Solution

In the first novel in the Truman and Celeste series, Truman stumbles into a detective gig and Celeste works her contacts in the art world as they wrangle with a series of lowlifes and some toxic secrets.

truman.dagmarmiura.com

For Position Only

In the second novel in the Truth, Lies and Love in Advertising series, Craig Keller, a wealthy Los Angeles advertising magnate, is forced to face his demons or lose the woman he loves.

adeleroyce.dagmarmiura.com

www.ingramcontent.com/pod-product-compliance
Lightning Source LLC
Chambersburg PA
CBHW010349170726
48284CB00011B/2843